Ariel Dorfman, born in Argentina, is a Chilean citizen who was forced into exile after the coup of 1973 that overthrew Salvador Allende. He is the author of *How to Read Donald Duck* and *The Empire's Old Clothes*, both nonfiction; the novels *Mascara, The Last Song of Manuel Sendero,* and *Widows; Last Waltz in Santiago and Other Poems of Exile and Disappearance*; and the plays *Widows* and *Reader*. His books have been translated into twenty languages.

A professor at Duke University, Dorfman is a regular contributor to *The New York Times*, the *Los Angeles Times*, *The Nation*, and *The Village Voice*. He lives with his wife and two sons in Durham, North Carolina, and in Santiago, Chile.

Praise for My House Is On Fire:

"The horrible dislocations in the normal human order are brilliantly and forcefully portrayed in every story in the collection. . . . Dorfman has been called the moral conscience of his country. The stories in *My House Is On Fire* attest powerfully to both the strength of his witnessing and the imaginative brilliance of his art. These stories have resonance and timeliness, a rare combination that makes them universal; they are political fables in the best sense."

—Don Skiles, *San Francisco Chronicle*

"Of all the Latin American writers to come out of that explosion of creativity familiarly known as 'el boom', Ariel Dorfman is the one whose work I love best. . . . He pushes the outer limits of the fictional envelope as daringly and imaginatively as Julio Cortázar and Gabriel García Márquez. . . . But what makes Dorfman's books especially appealing is the humanism of his vision."   —Wendy Smith, *The Cleveland Plain Dealer*

"The voices are assured, heartbreaking, and are bearing witness to an all-encompassing social suffering. . . . Finally, it is the generosity and sadness of *My House Is On Fire* that stays with the reader, that accepting of what has been done to us, of what we have done to ourselves."

—Jim Shepard, *The Washington Post Book World*

MY HOUSE
IS ON FIRE

ARIEL DORFMAN

Translated from the Spanish by George Shivers with the author

PENGUIN BOOKS

PENGUIN BOOKS

Published by the Penguin Group

Viking Penguin, a division of Penguin Books USA Inc.,

375 Hudson Street, New York, New York 10014, U.S.A.

Penguin Books Ltd, 27 Wrights Lane, London W8 5TZ, England

Penguin Books Australia Ltd, Ringwood, Victoria, Australia

Penguin Books Canada Ltd, 2801 John Street, Markham, Ontario, Canada L3R 1B4

Penguin Books (N.Z.) Ltd, 182–190 Wairau Road, Auckland 10, New Zealand

Penguin Books Ltd, Registered Offices: Harmondsworth, Middlesex, England

First published in the United States of America by Viking Penguin,

a division of Penguin Books USA Inc., 1990

Published in Penguin Books 1991

10 9 8 7 6 5 4 3 2 1

"Reader" first appeared in *Salmagundi,* "Trademark Territory" in *The Mississippi Review.*

LIBRARY OF CONGRESS CATALOGING IN PUBLICATION DATA

Dorman, Ariel.

My house is on fire/Ariel Dorfman; translated from the Spanish

by George Shivers with the author.

p.   cm.

ISBN 0 14 01.4728 4

I. Title.

[PQ8098.14.O7M9   1991]

863—dc20   90–7794

Printed in the United States of America

Set in Garamond No. 3

Designed by Michael Ian Kaye

Contents

These
stories
are for
María
Angélica,
who was
simply
there.

FAMILY CIRCLE

ORESTES: Don't expect to have a more faithful friend than I.

ELECTRA: Foreigner! Would you mock my misfortune!

ORESTES: I would be mocking my own.

> Aeschylus,
> *The Libation Bearers*

AGAMEMNON: Even so, you will have to sail, and then you'll remember your father.

IPHIGENIA: Will I be sailing with my mother or alone?

AGAMEMNON: Alone. Without either your father or your mother.

> Euripides,
> *Iphigenia at Aulis*

Any sonofabitch would have better luck than I do. The first bus I take in a year and instead of María Eugenia, who should be the one and only member of the reception committee sitting there on the bench at the bus stop no less, as if he knew that I was on the bus? Who should be giving the fucking eye to every sonofabitch passenger who got off? Who, huh?

Up until a year ago I would've jumped off the bus while it was still rolling; I would've let go with some war whoops that would've burst the eardrums of every living soul on the other side of the hill; and what a hug me and the old man would've given each other.

But now all I had to do was see him through the window as the driver came to a stop and I could tell by his stiff expression and the way his legs were sprawling that today had gone just as badly as yesterday and the day before and every other day of the month I had been away, that his legs had been holding out since dawn looking for a job that not only no one wanted to give him but that, with things as bad as they'd been lately, nobody even had to offer. All I had to do was see him there, that stern, somber hulk, leaning against the back of the bench, and I started feeling like a real piece of shit all over again, so uncomfortable right from the start that I almost considered the idiotic alternative of staying on the bus and going back to the barracks, which at that point was obviously impossible, but any wild idea occurs to you at a time like that, anything not to have to face the old man before I had a chance to talk things over with María Eugenia.

Any sonofabitch could beat my luck! The old man would've had to have a pact with the devil to have known that I was coming on that particular bus, because I hadn't even known it myself, since up until a little while before, my leave was supposed to start tomorrow, Saturday, in the morning, and I had thought, during the train trip, that I would walk home like always, just to save a few cents, for all the good they'd do me.

But there I was in the street in front of the station, with that heat that was determined to do me in right there on the spot shrinking my pores and drying up my arteries, and it was like I couldn't get my breath, I was so anxious to see my family right then, and there came that beautiful little bus, rolling up like a red temptation, with its windows maliciously wide open, and just thinking about it, in pure pleasure, I could feel the breeze already rewarding my hot neck and cooling my face, turning my throat into a crystal-clear waterfall, and loneliness was roasting me so bad I thought I'd never come out of it, and then I leaped on like an acrobat, like somebody mounting a warhorse, I leaped on, what else was I going to do? It was impossible to explain all this to the old man for the simple reason that the old man wasn't speaking to me, not a single, solitary syllable for the last seven months. But he still knew me better than I knew myself: in mid-afternoon he had sniffed out my act of treason against the family economy, even before I committed it and consequently had chosen to point his shoes in the precise direction of this bus stop to witness, judge and condemn the appearance of the black sheep of the family. It could have been María Eugenia. That peach of a girl—her eyes, as moist and soft as a mirror, happy where mine were melancholy— could have been the one who ripened into my welcoming committee. Why the hell wasn't she the one there, her hoarse little stream of a voice full of greetings and gossip? She could've been the one to guess instead of him, couldn't she?

Or mama. It was mama, after all, who had given me the dough a month ago. A bill so wrinkled it looked like she had been saving it since prehistoric times. I didn't want to take it from her. It seemed crazy to me. For the girls, I said. For milk or tea. But she stubbornly insisted; she stuck that good old bill in my hand as a farewell offering. As though that cunning old lady realized that no doubt I'd be bringing back some miserable news from the regiment; and in those cases, the best thing is to hurry it along, there's no enemy worse than sadness to keep you company during a hostile hike of several miles. For the bus, the old lady had insisted. So you'll come back soon. Keep it for the old man, I protested, trying to return it. For you, she corrected me.

I waited for the rest of the passengers to get off, and only then, when the driver turned around and looked at me like I was some kind of leper, did I decide to disembark.

The old man saw me right away, but for all the importance he gave to the event, it might have been a stone that got off the bus. He must have been surprised, but he didn't give so much as a sign of recognition. He let the people disperse, so the two of us were there separated by a few feet of emptiness and silence, as if somebody were filming us and I were a criminal just arriving in town and waiting for the right moment to draw my pistol and blow him away. A minute must have passed, maybe less, and only then did he deign to raise his eyes from the ground to examine me, or, I should say, to examine my uniform. Because, as for me, Lucho, it was like I wasn't even there; he just wanted to fasten that eagle eye of his on every last inch of my patriotic soldier rags. He took his time, looking me over from top to bottom, like morning inspection, or as if I had no more life than some mannequin in a showcase in a military museum. That's the way coat hangers must feel. I didn't know where to hide myself, what to do with the uniform, I felt like tearing it off then and there and hoped we'd both disappear as quickly as possible. I held on to my duffel bag and tried out a few words.

"Hi there, papa," I said to him. "How's things around here?"

Still not standing up, not taking his eyes off me, he started to slowly brush off his pants. First he patted the right leg and a fine spray of yellow dust rose. He kept on working on his pants right down to his shoes, never taking his eyes off me, while the dirt fell away like dry bubbles, all the dirt that had accumulated during his fruitless day of searching in factories, standing in line with the rest of the jobless, just to stand in another line five hours later, then the mansions up in the posh neighborhoods to see if they needed someone to cut the grass or to wash windows or to walk the dog, finally the municipal gardens just in case some friend who had managed by hook or crook to get into the minimal employment plan might be able to help him out, and from time to time a trip through the downtown area, full of roving beggars and well-stocked stores, from pillar to post, walking the city like a pariah. It was as if the old man had crossed the Sahara. He was carrying enough dust to smother an army. Then he repeated the whole operation with the left leg. There wasn't even the hint of a breeze in the midst of that infernal heat, so the dust just hung there, dizzy, orphaned of any support, floating in that withered air, until it would fall by its own inertia, reabsorbed by the pants, the shoes, the ground.

That was the moment to jump into the match, to spit out a ton of dust from every cell of my being, to dig it out even from under my tongue, but just this afternoon I was as clean as the day I was born, I didn't have a single glorious drop of sweat, not one sign of suffering, not even a gnarled throat to offer. I could have laid the bad news on him, of course; I could have explained that I was here on a Friday and not on a Saturday because the worst thing that could happen had happened, the thing that we had been expecting silently for months, but I had a feeling that wasn't going to stir up any pity in the old man. On the contrary, it was more likely that he would be overcome with rage, like a mad colonel, and would lay his curse on me then and there forever. So I coughed once, twice, three times, to see if that would at least loosen the knot in my throat and allow me to share with him, if nothing else, the dryness of this wasteland in which we were stuck, to see if it would remind him, even if remotely, that I had spent the whole damned year swallowing dirt, facedown, with my nose in a hole, practicing war exercises under the command of an all-powerful animal of a sergeant, on the receiving end of kicks by the dozens, lonelier than a skeleton, eating shit. Wasn't that enough for him?

The old man stood up suddenly and, like an officer, beckoned with his head for me to follow him. A sign that at least some bond still joined us. He didn't need to tell me that the distance that separated us at this moment was perfectly fine, that I should keep that distance, at least six feet between him and me, as if a contagious disease were hanging in every scandalous pocket of my uniform. He didn't need to tell me; because he had already made it brutally clear every time I had come back for a visit, in every one of the seven months since that night when I had decided that I couldn't avoid the draft, and I had to show up the next day for military service. As for María Eugenia, she could walk arm-in-arm with me, as embarrassing as that was not only to him and the family, but in fact to the town and the party and to the country as a whole. As for him, he at least had a little dignity left and he wasn't about to let anybody throw it up to him that he had consented to walk in public with or even close to an accomplice of those murderers and traitors and the worst sons of bitches the world had ever produced, so I should stay six feet, nine feet, a thousand feet, a thousand miles behind, if possible; I was not to speak to him as long as I was wearing those clothes. At least he hadn't burned all the bridges; he had left the door open to reconciliation once my military service was over. I knew his instructions by heart, so I didn't think of even approaching his shadow. When I saw his back at a prudent distance, I started following him.

The only hope left to me was that we would still come across María Eugenia, and she would alter the situation with one tempestuous toss of her dark hair. She was a real princess, even capable of taking me by one arm and the old man by the other and dragging us up the hill. She paid him no mind at all. From the very first day she proclaimed to the four winds that papa was wrong, and that nobody could refuse to do military service, that it made no sense for somebody to get himself shot just like that, and that, besides, a year goes by fast. It was her influence that kept the old man from closing the house to me completely. So now I was counting on María Eugenia's charm to find the old man's weak spot and to confront him at the proper moment with the little problem I was bearing. It would take her less than two minutes to convince me things weren't that bad. She would grab my head, looking for gray hairs. Old dog, she'd say to me, you were born old and sad and worn out, and you're still not twenty-one. I'm going to pull out your gray hairs for you, so you'll stop all these crazy thoughts. That was the way she cast sorrow aside: with belly laughs, practical jokes, tickling, dances running over with vitality. That's the way it had always been; it was as if she had been given all the joy and all I got was the uncertainty. She always said that no problem was so important that it deserved even half a tear, not one iota of a tear, she would say. Difficulties just slipped off that pretty back of hers, passed her by; she simply refused to recognize that anything could be worth the worry. You're an old dog, a crafty old dog, she would say. That's why in the neighborhood they called her the Alka-

Seltzer Girl. Because of her bubbly nature, the bewitching sparkle in her eyes, that way she had of relieving sorrows by insisting that they didn't exist. She became a mascot for the neighborhood, for the union, for papa, for the Mothers Center, here comes Miss Super Vitamin, the potion that puts an end to grief and gets rid of rats, here comes our little Alka-Seltzer. And so she had kept on growing, like grass that instead of turning yellow just keeps getting greener.

I shut my eyes and imagined that when I opened them she would be standing in front of me.

But María Eugenia failed to appear.

The old man, on the other hand, didn't need her to change his mood. No sooner had he stepped into the shantytown than his attitude changed as if by magic, as if one of his dead friends had risen up within him like a well of spring water. His stride became long, determined, convincing. I saw the way he squared his shoulders, raised his head, drove out his own fatigue. Just as I always had, I automatically changed the rhythm of my own stride to match his, so that, even at that distance, the frozen abyss he had placed between us would remain. The old man crossed the shantytown like a ship that refuses to go down. No one would whisper behind his back that they had seen him defeated or even depressed. Forget it. He knew every child by name, and he greeted them all as he went, laughing, mussing their hair with his hand, kicking an old can, until he had a flock of kids following behind him. He had a kind word for everybody, lifted the spirits of each and every grand-mom with a joke, reminded neighbors, in passing, that tomorrow there was a meeting of the unemployed, congratulated one who had found work, made flattering remarks to the dark-eyed girls who came out to giggle at the doors of their houses. A half-smile played at his lips, somewhat tender, somewhat proud, perhaps epic.

That was my papa, that's the way I always wanted to remember him, that's the way I had grown up beside him. My papa, returning now from better streets, future or past, bursting with a combination of energy and calm that had nothing to do with that moment either, but rather had been inherited from other marches and other songs, for a moment an invisible banner seemed to unfurl in his hands, it wasn't just two feet striding there but thousands, my papa, sowing himself as he advanced. There was the old man, unbroken, as though he had never been in prison, as though he had never had to lower his eyes to the ground the day his boss had come back to the textile mill that the workers thought they had expropriated from him forever, as though all the corners in that city still belonged to him and his *compañeros,* the old man walking through town like a general celebrating a victory, almost as if the *compañero Presidente* were still alive and not buried in some hole in a forgotten cemetery by the sea. My old man. Except that back then he had held my hand, I had felt his magnificent shadow protecting me. The whole family had marched, not a single one missing, horizon to horizon, side by side. Shit, it was the same old man now, leaving a con-stellation of hope in his wake, raising the spirits of the doubters, renewing the confidence of the faithful, blowing on the most hid-den ashes until the flame was rekindled, my incredible old man, passing through the slum like an eagle. So much enthusiasm, so much generosity, and nothing for me.

I limited myself to being a spectator. I stopped every time he did and contemplated the scene as if it were unfolding on a screen. There I was, an anonymous intruder among the shacks where I had been raised, where I knew the heartbreaks and the satisfactions of each and every neighbor, the mysterious pleated skirts of every female, the lies and the bravado of every male, me, part of the landscape, the prescribed six feet of distance, too far from the circle of his holy words to be reached, to be included, to be shel-tered by them, me, a lamppost, a deflated balloon, a birthday cake that nobody put in the oven, a cactus, me, his soldier-boy son.

Till we got to the foot of the hill and he started to talk to no less a personage than Nilda Paredes herself. I liked her a hell of a lot; she'd been something of a sweetheart of mine and her lips proffered kisses like succulent grapes, while the warmth of her body against mine promised even greater and better and more marvelous things. And when I had come back for my first visit, she had told me, unbuttoning every button with her eyes, melting my lapels like ice, taking my breath away with every square inch of material, her unbelievably fragrant skin so far away: "With you?" she had said. "I wouldn't be seen on the same street with you . . ." And then those little muscles moving that glorious ass away from me as quickly as possible . . . And since then it was as if she had become papa's main ally, because she wouldn't even speak to me.

María Eugenia said that she was a fool and that I should pay no attention to her, that she was probably jealous because women like guys in uniform, and that in a few more months everything would return to normal. But what did María Eugenia know about love? What did she know about my glands? When she was always running around with a flock of guys in her wake and she wouldn't give the time of day to any of them? I couldn't wait to see her the day she fell head over heels for one of them and he gave her the brush; then we'd really cry on each other's shoulder.

They started to talk in low voices, and it was impossible to make out a word they were saying. At first I thought it would only be for a minute, but the time passed and there they were, still chewing the fat, stretching the whole thing out beyond the bearable. All of a sudden I caved in, my defenses came tumbling down, and every pore in my body was sick and dying. It was like he was the youth and I was the old man, as if I was the one who had worn out those endless avenues with my goings and comings, returning with empty pockets, and he was the one who had gotten off the bus ablaze with a look of relaxation worthy of better times, as if he were Nilda's guy and I were some sterile, worn-out rival, so at that point I had no choice but to pull out of the show, to get away from there that very instant and go on ahead to see mama and my sisters, hugging the old lady for fifteen eternal minutes, feeling the way her arms understood me, her fingers, her heartbeat, her touch, feeling the buzzing warmth of the girls, still in awe of the family's only male child, all fluttering around me. Then a long walk with María Eugenia, with no need to explain anything, not even to fill in the lost experiences of this month of separation, not even to compensate with words for the weeks in which we hadn't seen each other, going on with the song as if the two of us had been humming it soundlessly all this time under water and it was enough to come up for air at the same moment to recapture the shared melody. Let Nilda and papa go on gossiping till Judgment Day, if they wanted to. I was splitting.

I grasped the handle of my duffel bag tightly, and remembered for just an instant Nilda's pretty neck, a little gazelle she was, and without so much as a good-bye, I turned and marched up the hill. Papa seemed to take note of my absence, he seemed to realize that his one-man audience had abandoned the stadium without waiting to see the winning goal, because no more than twenty seconds had passed when I sensed that he was behind me. The hill was steep and the old man was panting like a buffalo, stumbling, catching himself, hurrying to catch up with me, so I would see him there again at the head of the column, as always the town's main man, union leader in spite of all, as strong as an oak, as daring as a guitar, wiser than the sea. But I had already seen enough: I moved on at full speed. He followed my example, and I didn't want to lose any time looking to see how he would take advantage of every secret little path in order to regain the lost yards. It was a question of putting on the steam, of showing him that I had learned something as a recruit, and besides, I could take advantage of my unsurpassable knowledge of the terrain, because only María Eugenia knew this hill as well as I did. Every pebble, every little lizard, every bush was my friend. This was my wild kingdom and I was the prince, so the old man was going to have to be a wizard to beat me. As if he had overheard my thoughts, he responded by pushing to the limit those long legs the Lord had given him, assuming a measured and sustained trot, and finally, casting all dignity to the winds, he shifted to something between a run and a hop. The challenge was clear: it was a matter of who would get home first.

For an instant, I found myself taken back to my childhood. How many times had we repeated this same race back then? How many times had I waited for him on Friday afternoons outside the factory and experienced the fantastic relief of seeing him appear, so tall and so sure of himself, laughing among his *compañeros?* Your mother sent you, he would announce in that gently booming voice of his, to be sure all the money gets home. Right, champ? Not all of it, papa, I would answer, let's buy an ice cream cone first. And no doubt about it, there would be a triple dip when we got off the bus, and only after I had made short work of it, right there on that same bench where he had been waiting for me today, would he point to the house at the top of the hill and the figures of mama and María Eugenia probably waiting there, and would solemnly announce that he would get there before me, that now we'd see who was champ. I had to suppose that he would let me win, would allow me to cross the finish line a few minutes ahead of him, and I'd get first prize—a kiss from mama—but you could never be sure, once in a while he'd pass me, just so there'd be some suspense the next time.

But that isle of childhood had evaporated, and in its place there were two overgrown men, cursing and tripping up the hill like a couple of drugged horses, climbing it as though their lives depended on the outcome of that race, with no thought to what the neighbors would think. At first I didn't even look behind me, so as not to lose my advantage, and I swung my arms the way he had taught me to make my legs move faster, but really I was so far ahead that I needn't have worried. Besides, I was in better shape than he was; I exercised every day; they had me working like a well-oiled machine; those muscles that Nilda scorned were anybody's dream; and to top it all off, every Wednesday they took us out to scale a hill just like this one and whoever was the last one up ran the gauntlet and got a round of kicks in the butt from everybody else. So, as the old man lost ground and his breathing got heavier and heavier, my rage started ebbing away, and while my heart raced, my head started cooling off and I understood in a lightning flash of adulthood that I had to slow down, imperceptibly so he wouldn't notice, as if I were the grandfather who had to nourish the pride of his grandson. What was the pleasure in winning if I had arrived fresh and rested, but he was screwed? So I let him catch up with me and we reached the house with him a couple of feet in front, panting and out of breath, sweat pouring off him and on the point of collapsing, almost a draw, father and son, almost a draw.

Both of us leaned against the wooden wall and there we stood, like a couple of drowning victims waiting for first aid, and then I had the idea to brush off my pants the way he had done, first the right leg and then the left one, and now there really was a mushroom cloud of dust, precious dust from our hill, and then something like an "It's Sunday and I can rest all day" smile played at the corners of his mouth and I kept on beating out the dust as if it were gold, as happy as a lark, and he set to with his own pants and with all that dust we started to cough like a pair of TB patients and even some smothered laughter emerged from down deep in him, and though he still didn't say anything to me, not even that he could still beat me, it was clear that a little bit of the ice between us had melted, that by one of those miracles that occur between the peace-lovers of this world, things were not as bad as they had been and that you only had to turn up the heat a little to find that the same old affection and camaraderie were still there.

Then, to top it all off, the door of the house opened and mama came out, accompanied by an unmistakable aroma, an impossibly good aroma, one I hadn't smelled around there in I didn't know how long, the supernatural scent of chicken soup, cooking over a low flame. It hit me right here, a clip to the chin. Our mouths watered, as we anticipated what it would be like to dig into that pot. Tender carrots, potatoes cooked to a T, a generous sprinkle of coriander, parsley, green peas, and if it was a real banquet, some out-of-this-world corn and chicken that would melt in your mouth; and all of that took us on a toboggan ride to an earlier time, as if our race had started today and ended yesterday, landing us on some beach from the past, when the old man had a job, when things were cheap, when the old lady took in washing, when María Eugenia was getting prepared maybe even for the university, and everything was going a little better, a lot better, and once in a while we could indulge in the luxury of a meal like this one. So I closed my eyes to erase everything else and I hugged the old lady as if she were the very chicken who had died for that soup; I let the anticipated joy of that nocturnal menu that we would share as a family plug into every little corner of my chest, and allowed my tongue, my teeth, my throat, even my intestines to take off at a gallop, and for one feverish moment I think I even succeeded in abolishing the certainty that this weekend was going to be one of the blackest of my life, that I was going to have to tell the old man about that business, that this time we really would come to blows. I didn't dare ask myself how that wily old lady had managed to get together the money for that feast, because such witchcraft only happened in a month of Sundays; I just allowed myself to be cradled by the aroma of that fabulous soup, by the robust body of my jewel of a mother, by the honeyed fatigue of the race recently run. The only thing missing was the old man's voice calling for la Negra to go for a good bottle of white wine, that Lucho had come back home and the family was together again and this was cause for a hell of a celebration.

But when the old man spoke, it wasn't to announce any such thing. On the contrary, his voice filled with gravel, and even without looking at him it was clear that the smile had turned sour on his face, that the tension, which I had thought was about to melt away, had come back with a vengeance, hardening his jaws. I pictured him behind me, stiff and hostile.

"When you're finished"—my father's mouth directed his words to the old woman—"tell the soldier boy to change his clothes, okay? It's enough having to put up with so many uniforms in the streets; I won't have one in my house!"

I let go of mama as if a sword had been shoved between us. I took a deep breath and then something inside me decided not to go into the house, not to obey his orders.

"How are the girls?" I asked without turning around to see the old man's belligerence, trying to rescue whatever I could from the catastrophe, to reestablish that pot of food between mama and myself, the girls next to mama and me and la Negra.

"They're fine, thanks," she answered, but her voice was weak, as if she were talking over the phone. "They're all fine, thank God."

"I'm going to look for them," I announced. "Are they around here?"

The old lady wouldn't get off that goddamned nonexistent phone: "Off playing. Around here someplace, playing as usual. Didn't you see them as you were coming up?"

I chose each word carefully. "Didn't see them," I said. "But they're fine—that's what's important."

"They're great, as wild as ever, thank God. They'll turn up as soon as they know you got here today. We expected you tomorrow."

I swallowed.

"And how's la Negra?"

"Your sister's not here," said mama. "So, what happened, that they let you go on a Friday, son?"

How could I explain it, with the old shit there, listening, scrutinizing every word as if through a keyhole, capturing every word in flight to see if it carried some hidden meaning? Only María Eugenia could sweeten up the words so the old man would swallow them whole.

"When's she coming?"

"Who?" asked the old lady.

"María Eugenia."

The old woman wiped her hands on her apron. She looked at papa. "Well, I guess I don't even have to ask you how things went, because it's clear they went badly."

"Better not to ask," the old man confirmed.

She sighed, deeper than necessary. "Come on in and wash up, men. You both look a fright. Racing, at your age. I saw you; I was watching my two marathon boys."

"Good idea," the old man said. "A little water never hurt anybody."

"That can wait," I said. "I'm going to look for María Eugenia. Where is she, mama?"

The old man's words fell on me like a ton of bricks, a slap in the face, crushing me like some miserable bug.

"So he thinks that can wait? I'm glad that's clear, that we know his opinion. Of course, since the soldier boy had his magnificent shower in the barracks, and then took a bus because his patriotic legs are too delicate to walk, why should he wash? Right? But I will, yes sir. I will. Florencia, go draw me some water."

"Mama," I insisted. "Where is María Eugenia?"

"She went out."

"Then I'll go down to wait for her. When did she say she'd be back?"

"She didn't say," she answered. "But it's going to be late. You'd better go on in and change clothes like your father asked and then rest awhile. The girls will be coming in soon and we're going to eat."

I was once more engulfed by the aroma of the soup. I not only smelled it; it wafted over my skin, I could almost touch it, could almost hear and see its texture, as it blended with my breath like some living, bloody wind.

"Late?" I asked. "Where did she go?"

"She didn't say," mama repeated.

We were interrupted by shrieks of savage joy down the hill. Papa pointed with his finger and changed, as though by a miracle. "Here come those devils. Look at that! Would you look at how those damn girls can run!"

The three of them were coming up the hill like mountain goats. Each one was dressed in a different color and it was great watching them jumping, swinging their arms like propellers, shouting at me to look at them, spinning around like tops, and then rising up in splendor, first imitating Tarzan of the Apes and then Cheetah, the chimpanzee, and finally a herd of buffalo, a regular hurricane of boundless energy, their long hair flowing, dark and clean. Really, they were great; mama was absolutely right: so different from my last visit. Then they had seemed so tired, drowsy, lifeless and, yes, of course, hungry.

Then mama's voice floated out softly: "Didn't I tell you they were fine? Do you see? At least now they're eating." But there was something so remote and stormy in her tone, a melancholy bite that stuck there and remained unreconciled to the delight of those words, something so worn and savage that all of a sudden I was afraid; I had to contain the wave of fear that swept over me like a grease stain.

For an instant it was still possible to ignore that note of intense bitterness in the old lady's message, and I was able to control my own panic. Like my parents, like mama and papa, I fixed my gaze, as if we were watching the girls from some open window in a picture taken years before, admitting to ourselves the joy of that hill being conquered by those three loud and glorious little savages, my own eyes as suddenly innocent as the girls themselves. Just a while back it had been us, the twins, María Eugenia and Lucho, who greeted the old lady as she carried the unborn Patricia; we were the ones who calmed the afternoon heat with our shouts.

But that was the final truce; that spell, that magical isle where we had managed to establish a transitory residence, couldn't last. María Eugenia was not present, neither up here with us nor down there with them. Before those three elves arrived, before anything else—washing or eating or hugging or crying or breathing—I had to find out what had happened to her. I knew what I was going to do, but I didn't think I had the nerve. I planted the question.

"And the money, mama? Where did the money come from?"

It was the old man I was really asking, and with terror I realized that he was going to answer me directly, that he would no longer use mama as a bridge; I understood it by the way he dragged his gaze away from the exuberant advance of the girls, by the way he was turning to me, I knew that there was no escape; for the first time since I had joined the army he was going to speak to me, head on, face-to-face, man to man, as they say, and I wished I had

cut out my tongue rather than ask that question and that I had
stones in my ears in order not to hear the answer and that I'd never
been born, never drawn a single breath in this world, never scaled
this damned hill, never arrived with María Eugenia on the same
day to this house where papa and mama were waiting, where now
this answer was waiting.

"So you want to know where the money came from?" asked
papa, in a low voice. "You really want to know?"

"I wash," said mama. "Mrs. Menéndez called on us to help her
with the housework."

Where did the old man get the strength to talk to me like that,
so calmly? From what rampart was he speaking? What land? What
cavern floor supported his feet?

"Lucho," he said. And I stepped back so he couldn't place his
hands on my shoulders, so his voice couldn't reach me; I stepped
back toward the house. "You're going to have to ask your sister.
She's the one who found work."

"She sleeps in," mama intervened. "Mrs. Menéndez has been
very good to us and says that María Eugenia can stay the whole
week."

And far off, farther away than the Indian war whoops of the
three little animals coming up the hill, I heard my own voice; it
was my own voice that was saying:

"Where does she work, old man? Where?"

His eyes revealed neither pain nor rage nor hope nor anything
else; they were void of all victory and all defeat, empty, indifferent,
motionless, entirely there. He didn't answer my question. He only
said:

"You're going to have to ask her that, Lucho."

"I'm not going to ask her; I'm asking you."

He took a step toward me, as if he were going to hit me or take
me in his arms.

"Don't come any closer," I shouted. "Tell me when she's coming
back. I want to know when she's coming back."

He stood still.

"Tomorrow," said my father. "You can ask her tomorrow morning."

With great care, excessive, infinite care, I laid my duffel bag on
the ground.

"I'm not going to ask her anything," I said. "I've got nothing to ask her."

"Then don't do it," he said. "You've made your own decisions up to now. It's your affair. As for me, I'm going in to wash up a little before supper . . . Old woman, will you heat a little water for me?"

I walked to the door before he did.

"So you like chicken, huh, papa? You must be really hungry, right?"

He answered firmly:

"I'm a little hungry, yes. Like everybody else." I didn't wait another minute. Containing myself so as to hide the trembling of my legs and my arms, I went in the house. The old lady followed me, faster than a passing chill. There it was. There was the pot, in the shadows, over the sputtering flame. On the table there was bread, a bottle of milk, even a little goat cheese. I measured my movements, hoping my hands would obey me. I picked up the pot. It was heavy, and the hot metal bit into my hands like a mad dog. But from inside rose that delirious aroma of the angels, that essence of a mother cooking for her family, of evenings long past and of a full house, of *compañeros* from work, visitors, foremen, all stopping by to say hello, of all the aunts and uncles and cousins and of a grandmother who had died.

"So, María Eugenia filled up the pot, huh?"

The old lady didn't answer. She just stood in the doorway. She almost blocked the light.

"Mama," I said. "Get of the way. Let me pass."

She spoke slowly and hoarsely, so that only I could hear her, so that nobody else in the whole universe could guess what she was saying.

"Not the food, Lucho. Put it back. Right now."

The hot metal was burning my hands to a crisp. The pain was unbearable. But I wasn't about to let go, not even if my fingers were smoking.

From behind mama loomed the old man's powerful silhouette. He blinked, trying to adjust his eyes to the semi-darkness. Then he tried to enter the room, but she didn't budge.

"That's what they've taught him in the army," he whispered in mama's ear, but I could hear him chewing every word and spitting them out like darts. "That's what the soldier boy has learned." He tried to push mama out of the way. "Let me in right now, Florencia."

She settled into the doorway even more. "Lucho, put that pot down," she said.

I paid no attention. I concentrated on holding back the cries of pain that were rising from my hands, devouring my arms and threatening my heart. I lifted the pot higher, with a superhuman effort.

"Are you hungry, old man?" I asked. "Really hungry?"

"The girls are," he said. "Me, just a little. But the girls are. Less than before, though."

My whole body was on fire; it was as if my hands no longer existed, as if somebody had grabbed them and was torturing them in some cellar. All of a sudden I shouted like a madman, so that the whole hill, the neighborhood, the city could hear me, so that he would hear me and never forget.

"I'm being transferred, old man. To Ritoque. Ritoque—do you understand? I'll be a guard there, in Ritoque. I'll watch the prisoners. Are you listening, old man?"

My mother reacted before he did. "Ritoque," she said. "Do they know that your uncle, that Roberto is there?"

"They're transferring me. That's what I came to tell you. They're sending me to Ritoque."

The old man half-pulled, half-pushed mama, and struggling, managed to get into the room. But he stayed in the doorway; he didn't go on to where I was waiting for him. Once again, there we were, six feet from each other, separated by an empty space like two movie cowboys. Then he hurled the same question at me that he had asked so many months ago; it was like an echo twisted in a mirror; that time I announced to him that my number was up, that there was no escape, that my name was there on the list in black and white and I was going to have to go.

"So, what are you going to do?" the old man asked me then and was asking me now.

But this time María Eugenia was not there to answer him, to drum a little common sense into his head, to explain. What could I do? What kind of damned question was that? Go, of course, you hardheaded old man! When an order was given, you had to go; you had to obey or they'd stick a bayonet up your ass. What else could I do?

The peppery steam from the pot got in my eyes and tears started to flow. I felt like a torch, as if I were descending into Hell in a slow elevator.

"They're transferring me, old man," I said almost imperceptibly. "To Ritoque."

Then papa crossed the space that separated us and put both enormous hands on the pot. Gently he tried to take it from me, to lift it. I felt the weight growing less, the suffering of my hands being soothed, but I made one last effort and clung to it, to that unbearable heat. The hot, violent liquid splashed out, greasy, at our feet. Our pants were sprayed, but neither of us moved.

"Okay," he said. The aroma from the pot engulfed us both like a sacred mist. Gradually his hands took charge of it. "It's not hard to help the *compañeros* who are prisoners. You can always think of ways to give them a little hand, pass along a message, offer a little support. Right?" And his hands moved implacably over the metal, they must be burning by now; it must be singeing his skin, sinking to the bone; his blood had to be boiling.

I hugged the kettle with all the strength I had left.

"Listen to me! I want to tell you something, papa. Just one thing."

Outside the voices of the girls grew louder; they would burst through the door at any moment. One heavy, warm, salty tear slid down to my mouth. I felt the kettle slipping; I was going to have to drop it.

There was his face, directly in front of me. I had never had him so close in my life.

"I'm telling you they're not going to catch me, papa. If I can help, okay. But first things first. They're not going to catch me."

"That comes first. And what about second?"

I allowed every syllable to be heard in the silence.

"The second thing is that if somebody tries to escape, I'll shoot him. Whoever it is, I'll kill him if he tries to escape while I'm on guard duty. I'll shoot him full-blast. Is that clear?"

"Is that the way they say it?" asked the old man. "Full-blast?"

"I want to know if what I'm saying is clear."

And then I had to let go of the pot; I had to leave it in his hands, that were waiting for it as though it were a newborn baby, as though some secret force were protecting that pot. My hands hung at my side like a pair of burned birds.

"That seems clear enough," he said. He gestured toward the door with his head, toward what must be the beginning of twilight, down the hill. "And it should also be clear that tomorrow morning you're going with me to the bus stop to wait for your sister, right? You and I are going to get up early, go together. Or do you plan to let María Eugenia come home without anyone to accompany her?"

I didn't answer.

At that moment the girls came in like a sea of light, like three little doves in a sea of light. But they left the noise outside; I was moved by so much wisdom in such children. It was as if they were entering a church or arriving late at a funeral. They stood watching us, in silence. I tried not to look at them.

The old man put the kettle back on the stove, calmly, taking his time. He placed both hands on his hips and stared at me.

Since the silence was growing heavy, mama spoke up.

"All right," she said. "Now we're all here. You must be hungry, Lucho. How about if I prepare supper?"

I didn't answer for a while. I didn't know what to do with my eyes, but I ended up staring at him, at the old man, my father, standing there like a demon or like a saint beside the pot.

"Yes, mama," I said, not a tear in my voice, not allowing my throat to betray me for one damned minute. It was a good idea, a great idea. "I'm starving."

READER

He had hardly begun to read the manuscript that Friday morning when he knew he was going to have to censure it.

As might be expected, the references to the regime were not explicit. If it had just been a question of a word here and there, then all he would have to do was scratch out the offending language, suppress a few passages, change some meanings and, finally, authorize conditional publication. But that wasn't the case. That novel, *Turns,* was a devastating, merciless, head-on attack on the government, its venality, corruption, repression.

Don Alfonso was amazed that his friend Bergante, the editor, would ask him even to consider the book. According to the law prior approval was no longer strictly necessary, as it had been in periods of greater restrictions. Now books were judged after publication, and that policy turned publishers into relentless self-censors, since they didn't want to be left with thousands of copies mouldering in the vast, damp warehouses of the Information Ministry. If Bergante had decided to solicit Don Alfonso's opinion in advance, it must surely be that he believed the author's talent worthy of such consideration, but, on the other hand, felt that the book's acceptance by the authorities was problematic. He was right. Even an apprentice censor—and Don Alfonso had twenty years' experience in the office without a single mistake—would have realized that that book was hiding (and barely so; instead it seemed proud of its rebellion) an attack upon the fundamental principles of the State.

That was already clear by page thirty, yet Don Alfonso—who was, in general, not an impressionable man and, in fact, was known for his lightning-fast judgments beyond appeal—let himself be carried along by the soft spell of the prose, which was at once flexible, sensual and surprising, as if every word were in love with the way it sounded. He went on reading. The story took place during a hypothetical dictatorship in the year 8000 or thereabouts. Popular discontent had already reached enormous proportions and everyone could see the end in sight. The only thing lacking was a little pressure on some exposed nerve to coalesce the forces of the resistance and to precipitate the fall of the regime in power. Imperceptibly, the novel focused its attention on one bureaucrat in the administration, a rather dull fellow who occupied a minor position, but whose collaboration was essential to bringing down the government, for reasons that were still unclear. Or was it that this fellow symbolized the last point of support the government could hope for?

Don Alfonso started to feel somewhat annoyed at José Córdova (that was the official's name). He hadn't paid much attention to him at first. He was there more or less as a kind of mailman, just part of the background. But all of a sudden the character made a gesture. He scratched his left ear, and at that point Don Alfonso felt a small wild animal stir in the pit of his stomach.

"That man is me," he said out loud, and the sound of his own voice seemed unreal and empty in his office piled high with papers.

As a matter of fact, everything pointed to such an identification. Like him, that offical had lost his wife in a traffic accident at the age of thirty-one; he had had to take charge of a son whose studies, from then on, he supported by working as a public official in the mornings, while he had another job during the afternoons; and, to top it all off, he frequented the house of a possessive lover whose magnificent breasts offered a haven from boredom but whom he really did not love all that much. It was as if someone had transposed him onto those pages. When he got to the description of José Córdova—excessively detailed in a book where the author hardly bothered to do more than briefly sketch in his other characters—he almost lost his breath. Fiftyish, with a hooked nose, gray-green eyes, protruding cheekbones, a mop of hair where a tendency to grayness was carefully disguised, the habit of stepping heavily on one foot while slightly dragging the other: it was he. Yes, it could be no one else. He existed, came vibrantly alive, in the middle of that civilization which was supposedly thousands of light-years away.

"Just my luck," he thought with dry humor, recovering from what could only be one of Bergante's bad jokes. "Somebody I don't know finally notices me and immortalizes me in literature and he does it in a book that will never be published."

That was crystal clear, however much Don Alfonso might go on reading. Publication of that paean to subversion, that mocking attack on the authorities and their increasingly absurd exercise of power, would be interpreted, in the first place, as an inadmissible weakness of the regime. It would prove something that everyone already believed deep inside: the government was coming apart at the seams; it was not even capable of controlling its own administrative mechanisms and of holding on to the decisive support of the military. The book could not be published: not with reservations or temporary postponement; not authorized with changes and not even conditionally denied publication. Nothing. Prohibited forever and a day, in compliance with instructions from his superiors. That was that.

The telephone rang.

Don Alfonso had difficulty tearing himself away from his reading. At that very moment, José Córdova was being visited by his son, the one for whom he had made so many sacrifices, the one on whose behalf he had even accepted that degrading and miserable job. Ernesto had come to demand that he make a decision. Don Alfonso still did not understand what service José Córdova could render the resistance. Was it a matter of stealing an administrative file? Falsification of documents? Lying to his boss? Proving that someone whom the Ministry had declared dead was in fact lying in one of those labyrinthine, plastic prisons from the year 8000? This last alternative seemed to be strongly suggested, but he was not sure because all was insinuation, circumstance and double meaning.

"Old man," Ernesto was saying, "things can't go on like this."

The telephone persisted.

It was Bergante.

"So?" he said. "What do you think? Hard case, right?"

"If you're referring to *Turns*," Don Alfonso answered, "I was just reading it now."

"Hard case, right?" Bergante repeated.

"Hard indeed," Don Alfonso agreed, but not wanting to commit himself.

"The kid has exceptional talent. No doubt of that."

"I am not disputing his talent. Merely his politics."

"So there's no way, huh?"

Don Alfonso surprised himself. Instead of putting an end to the matter then and there, he said: "I still haven't finished. I haven't formed a definitive opinion."

"So it's impossible," Bergante stated. "I feared as much."

"I didn't say that," Don Alfonso replied. "There are, no doubt, difficulties that must be considered. Let me finish the manuscript."

"It's perfectly clear. I won't publish it. I'd just lose my investment, right?"

"Look, Bergante, I'm rather busy right now. Let me call you on Monday."

He decided not to go back to his reading. It was already late, the phone call had broken the novel's spell and several already published books required his verdict by noon. He left the manuscript open and immersed himself in *Mother Superior's Recipes: A Convent's Culinary Secrets,* and since he could find no problem, theological or otherwise, among those monastic sauces, he gave the book his stamp without further delay. He then turned his sharp eye to the use of the color yellow in frescoes recently uncovered in the ruins of Ur-Buk-Ka and concluded that the author—even if he were alluding to the transitory nature of this and every other authoritarian government—represented no immediate threat. That very afternoon the book would go into circulation with its abundant illustrations consisting of photographs by the archaeologist's wife.

Because Don Alfonso never erred. His nickname was "the Pope." The zeal he put into his work was not due to his boundless devotion to the government. In fact he didn't approve of certain aspects of official policy, the brutal treatment of prisoners, the massive unemployment. He had taken this job so that his son could become a doctor. But he was proud of his record, no mistakes, visible or invisible. It was a matter of honor. No book authorized by him had ever produced a scandal. No legal action had ever been initiated against a work he had approved. Once his permission had been issued no book had been confiscated. And it wasn't that he had no enemies. Envy of his reputation, not admiration, dominated the other censors. But they had never been able to pin an error on him. With his inexorable method, he undermined the sophistry of any author, any ambiguous or supposedly distant allusion; he explored the allegories, symbols and the subtlest contradictions. "Follow Don Alfonso's example," the Director of Censorship would say. "He's the one who authorizes the most books, and yet look, he has no demerits on his service record."

From time to time his colleagues would ask him how he did it, what his secret was.

"Very simple," Don Alfonso would reply. "There are three golden rules. In the first place, you have to have a method and stick to it. Second, you have to be implacable. In this business there is no room for feelings. Leave them at home! And in the third place, you have to be in tune with public taste." And then, he would add, from the heights of his administrative infallibility: "I almost forgot a fourth rule, one that cannot be learned. Culture, gentlemen. You must have culture."

It was that last piece of advice that the other censors couldn't forgive. Don Alfonso knew that his colleagues took turns carefully going over the books he had approved from cover to cover, with the not-too-veiled hope of finding some mistake. At the first slip, they would pounce on him like a pack of petty wolves, totally without culture, of course, but methodically, implacably and exquisitely in touch with public taste. They would have found some way to crucify him already, despite his excellent bureaucratic record, had it not been for the unrestricted support of the Director of Censorship.

Although Don Alfonso felt the urge to continue reading about the adventures and decisions of José Córdova, to discover what his son's request would be, curiosity did not influence his conduct that morning. His famous black pen continued its slow, unalterable labor. He accepted for publication a collection of poetry, replacing the word *lion* with *sheep* four times. *Approved with changes,* he wrote on the appropriate page. The book would have to go back to the printer, the pager and the linotypist. That should serve as a warning to the publisher. As for the reader, he would end up confused, unable to read any hidden political meaning into a text that seemed so incoherent. The beauty of the verses was not greatly altered.

And since he became immediately absorbed in an excellent novel—
which would never see the light of day because of its subversion
of good customs and of Christian morality—full of delicious por-
nographic insinuations, he hardly realized it when twelve o'clock
came and it was time to leave for his other job. He didn't have
time for even a brief glance at *Turns,* which remained on his desk
awaiting his judgment on Monday.

He felt relieved.

"With three swift kicks I'll dispatch José Córdova, his son Ernesto and the whole gang of subversives surrounding them," he
said to himself as he boarded the elevator.

There he found himself face-to-face with the Director of Censorship, who was also going down.

"What do you say, Don Alfonso? Hard as nails?"

"I try to carry out the delicate duties that have been assigned
to me."

His boss came closer and spoke in a low voice, even though they
were alone in the elevator.

"You must be even more careful now. The attacks are concentrating on our work. Our enemies are trying to undermine us."
He ended almost in a whisper. "We've got to authorize more works,
so they won't accuse us of thwarting democracy. But at the same
time we've got to authorize less, or they'll think we're growing
soft."

Outside it was raining. The Ministry's chauffeur was waiting for
the Director. He took his leave with a wave of his hand. "Hard as
nails, Don Alfonso. Okay? Don't let even a hint of subversion get
by you. The bastards have got us in their sights."

"You know me," said Don Alfonso, but the Director had already
departed.

It was then that he realized he was getting wet. He had left his
old umbrella upstairs, an uncharacteristic forgetfulness. He took
the elevator once again and when he had rescued that relic of long
ago, he was suddenly curious to take another look at the manuscript
that Bergante had recommended. There was the author's name on
the cover, along with his home address, just as the law required
in order to settle eventual responsibilities. No phone number. He
wrote down the information in his notebook, noting that the address was in one of the poorest neighborhoods in the city. He

would ask his son if he happened to know the man. Perhaps that would explain the strange coincidences between the text and his own reality.

But Enrique had never heard of anyone called Alvaro Parada. "Who is he?" he asked that night, when Don Alfonso mentioned the author in passing. "What does he do?"

"It seems that he writes," answered Don Alfonso, suddenly uncomfortable.

"If he's a writer then it would be up your alley, papa. Who mentioned the fellow to you?"

Don Alfonso was silent. He regarded his son with suspicion. Was he telling the truth? Or did he really know this author of subversive fiction? Had Enrique spoken to him sometime regarding his father's life and character and had these anecdotes found their way into the man's novel, consciously or unconsciously? Ernesto, José Córdova's son, was a master of deception. Was Enrique, too?

"Enrique, are you telling me the truth?"

It was a question he hadn't asked in many years.

"Papa!" Enrique protested.

But something in the timbre of Enrique's voice, in the quickness of his gesture of negation, in the sudden flush of his cheeks, disturbed his father. He felt dizzy, as though it were not his son there in front of him, but rather a perfect stranger who had assumed a mask. He suddenly said:

"You're involved in something, aren't you? You're involved."

"Something? I don't know what you're talking about."

"*Something* means politics. Don't play the innocent. I can see that you're set on ruining your medical career by behaving foolishly. What is it now? What is the nasty business?"

Enrique took a deep breath and opened his eyes wide the way he always had as a child when he wanted to be believed. "Can you tell me what this is all about? Does this interrogation have something to do with that author you just mentioned?"

Of course Enrique was up to something, just like Córdova's son in the novel. Don Alfonso had no doubt. His son was not about to confide in him, a loyal servant of the regime. He wanted to deter Enrique from such activity, to ask him to wait until he had finished his degree, until he had his diploma in hand. He thought about telling him that whatever happened, he could count on his father, that even if he didn't approve of violent activities or of the risks they involved, even if hard times came, the door of his father's room would always be open to him, but that he should be careful and choose his companions well, because it was a fact that all the regime's adversaries were not alike and . . .

He cut off his line of thought right there. Every bit of it could be called melodramatic, and besides, up to now there wasn't the slightest basis in reality for such hasty conclusions. It was that damned book that had upset him, stirring up doubts and creating problems where there were none. That was precisely why such texts should be banned. If he had finished it this morning, it wouldn't be spinning around in his head now, making insinuations and creating problems, as it had all afternoon.

"Nothing, son. Please forgive all this nonsense. You will agree that it isn't usual in me. I think I'm just especially tired today."

"Too much reading?" was the ironic reply. "You don't suppose you're turning into Don Quixote?"

Don Alfonso wished him a good night and went to bed.

Although he couldn't exactly remember when he woke up the next day, he had the impression he had dreamed about José Córdova (the man had his own face, but was not he, Alfonso), lost in an endless labyrinth of corridors in the year 8000. The only thing that stuck with him was that, at some point, standing in front of one of those doors that never opened along that endless hallway, he must have made a decision, because the first thing he did was to get up and check his notebook to be sure he had written down the address of the creator of *Turns*. He would go and see this Alvaro Parada; it would be easy enough to find out where he had come up with that character who was his own twin. He might even be able to find out if his suspicions about Enrique were justified. And he wouldn't have to wait until Monday to find out the rest of the story. It would be fun to hear from the novelist's own mouth the answer the bureaucrat José Córdova had given to his son.

"All the more reason to pay him a call," Don Alfonso said to himself, while he shaved, asking himself if, in the novel, José Córdova would have dared to intrude on the private life of a perfect stranger. "Nonsense," he added, and noted that his image smiled back at him from the mirror. "What do I care what that fellow would do?"

It took him a good hour and a half to get to the address. He had never been in that neighborhood. A shabbily dressed child pointed him in the direction of a muddy alley at the end of which stood a dilapidated apartment building. He climbed to the fifth floor and stood a minute to catch his breath. Without knowing why, he decided not to ring the doorbell right away, but rather to put his ear to the door: above the shouts of a veritable flock of children could be heard the irregular tapping of a typewriter.

The bell didn't work, so he knocked.

A woman opened the door. A long time ago she must have been attractive. She was wiping her hands on her apron. Three wide-eyed children peered out from behind her, modestly but cleanly dressed. The noise of the typewriter ceased. When the woman spoke, he noted profound fatigue in her voice.

"He isn't here," she said curtly. "You came to see him, didn't you?"

Don Alfonso improvised on the basis of a sudden intuition.

"I'm not a bill collector, madam. On the contrary, I'm here to talk to your husband about a matter that could be mutually beneficial."

She hesitated. She had acquired the deep wisdom of someone who often has to make snap judgments about the people who knock on the door. Don Alfonso felt her eyes penetrating to his very backbone, although it was only a glance, and then she stared at the floor.

"He isn't in," she pronounced finally. "If you like, you can leave your name and he'll call you when he returns."

"I'm a publisher," Don Alfonso declared. "A friend of Bergante. There's nothing to fear."

She still didn't believe him, convinced that something didn't fit, but at the same time she couldn't afford to stir up problems with any friend of Bergante's. Don Alfonso experienced a sudden discomfiture, but it was too late to back out now.

"Come in," the woman said and she opened the door. Her stern expression softened. It was as if she had put aside her watch-dog role, and something like a fountain of youth bubbled up from within her. "Come in," she repeated. "There he is, writing as usual . . . You understand that . . ."

"Of course, madam. You don't need to explain. It is I who should beg your pardon for invading your privacy with no warning, but since you don't have . . ." and he stopped what he was saying. She knew very well that they had no telephone. Why remind her? Once again Don Alfonso asked himself what had gotten into him, what he was doing there. He cleared his throat to hide his embarrassment. "Oh, no, no, it's just fine, perfectly fine."

The apartment was small, although not squalid. The woman little by little had arranged and decorated it. In the room where the three children probably slept, the beds were already made, but toys were scattered about the floor. The parents must sleep in the other, larger room which also served as a dining room and a living room and—what was unusual in such a place—a study. Alvaro Parada was seated at the table, surrounded by a veritable chaos of papers and with an antiquated Remington beneath his fervent and expectant fingertips, but he wasn't touching the keys, obviously to avoid revealing his presence to any undesired visitor.

He had hardly seen Don Alfonso when, instead of standing up to greet him, he hurled a "Just a moment!" and furiously attacked the sentence he had been working on when he heard the knocks at the door. "Just a moment. Just a moment," he went on murmuring, fully concentrating on the half-filled page. Then he became as absorbed in the typewriter as if he were playing a piano or making love to it, completely forgetting that Don Alfonso or the members of his own family existed.

"If I'm disturbing you . . . ," Don Alfonso ventured to say, but his own irritation had disappeared. He felt strangely well, standing there beside the woman and the children, watching the man work with such devotion and enthusiasm, totally absorbed in his magnificent fury. It was like getting on a bus in the dead of winter; with the heat inside and the rainy streets outside, you feel like passing your stop and indeed never getting off; just to let yourself doze off, rocked by the movement of the bus and the sensation of being in someone else's hands, the hands of people who knew where to go and why.

It seemed that the woman was not so happy.

"Dear," she interrupted his work, "this gentleman . . ."

"Ernesto," Don Alfonso hastened to explain, choosing the first name that came to his mind. "Ernesto Gacitúa, at your service, but it doesn't matter if . . ."

The woman went on in a firm, determined tone.

"Don Ernesto is a publisher and he wants to speak to you about . . . about important business. Your books."

"Just a minute," he said without taking his eyes off the page. "It's the burial scene. Only a minute. I'm almost finished."

"Excuse me," Don Alfonso insisted. "I can come back later."

"It's just that today is Saturday," she said, as if that explained everything. "Won't you sit down, please? Could I get you some coffee?"

"No, thank you, madam. You're very kind," Don Alfonso answered too quickly and was immediately ashamed, because she would think he was considering the fact that they would surely have little coffee and that perhaps it was a luxury they didn't even permit themselves. "Yes, thank you, that would be very nice," he corrected himself.

"It's Saturday," she insisted. "He works all week and besides, on Saturdays, grandfather goes out, so he has more peace and quiet. And in fact that's when I get the chance myself to read his manuscripts."

The man jumped up from the table. "All ready." He shook his hand and sat down in an ancient armchair which had been nicely restored. "You understand, if one leaves an idea half-finished, it's gone forever. Words are implacable."

"And characters?" Don Alfonso asked, resisting the need to scratch his left ear.

"They're worse," the man replied. "They never forgive. At this very moment I was trying to mix a scene in a cemetery with another one where the son of the man they are burying is born. If I don't write it the way I should, the fellow will rise from the grave and haunt me like a ghost. Characters are terrible, if you don't give them freedom."

Don Alfonso changed the subject. He mumbled an excuse for his so inopportune intrusion.

"Not at all. You're a publisher, you said. Gacitúa. Ernesto Gacitúa. Actually I never heard of anyone with that name who was in the business."

Seeing their father free of the Remington's terrible claws, the three children leapt upon him jubilantly. He didn't ask them to go outside and play or any such thing. He effortlessly transformed himself into a kind of miniature roller coaster they could ride, with the remark that they should be quiet in their game, because the grown-ups had things to talk about.

"I represent a firm which for the moment prefers to remain anonymous. Is that all right?"

"I prefer to know who I'm dealing with."

"To show that you can trust me," said Don Alfonso, "I will tell you that I have read part of your manuscript *Turns*."

Something sparkled in the writer's eyes, and it was as if his skin itself had brightened. "You read it? What do you think?"

Don Alfonso saw no reason not to give his firm judgment. "Admirable . . . but it seems difficult to have it published. You know how these things are . . ."

The other man answered with absolute calm, "I know very well how things are. They're going to change, of course, but in the meantime . . . I'm not surprised. There's no way the censors could let it pass."

"Oh," said Don Alfonso. "So our friend Bergante has already informed you about that?"

"Do you know Carlos Bergante?"

The woman interrupted, coming in at that moment with the coffee and two cups.

"That's why I invited the gentleman in . . . He comes recommended by Mr. Bergante."

Don Alfonso became alarmed. "Well, I wouldn't say a recommendation. In this business, we all know each other. In any case, I would prefer that you not mention my visit to him."

The writer placed two teaspoons of Nescafé and one teaspoon of sugar in his cup. He passed Don Alfonso the sugar bowl. "Bergante told me there was no chance. He had sent it to a fellow they call the Pope, he's infallible, they say, and he held out no hope at all."

"That's what he said? Well, but there must be other books of yours . . . Perhaps . . . my firm would be interested in them."

The woman pulled up a chair close to her husband's. Don Alfonso felt those eyes once again, scrutinizing him, sizing him up, trying to understand who he was, why he was there, what his intentions were.

"Don Ernesto," the writer said, "I want to be completely frank with you. I'm loyal, Don Ernesto. Carlos has gone out on a limb for me; he's argued with his associates on my behalf. He's the first one to have backed me."

"Has he done so disinterestedly?" asked Don Alfonso. "Or because he senses a thaw in the air, a relaxing of the regime?"

"I really don't care why he's doing it. I have learned to judge people by what they do and not by what they think. As long as he wants to publish my work and is fighting for my right to say what I have to say, I'm going to be loyal to him."

"Young man," Don Alfonso replied dryly, "you still haven't published a thing, and you're already planning your complete works. Doesn't that seem rather presumptuous to you?"

"If it weren't for this damned government!" he declared with sudden violence, and despite a frown from his wife, who nonetheless did not remove her penetrating eyes from Don Alfonso's face, he went on: "Yes, it's one shit of a government, and Don Ernesto agrees with me; if he didn't, he wouldn't be here. And it's not just Don Ernesto who thinks so; the whole country feels the same way. We've had it up to here. The government's a piece of super-shit, right?"

Don Alfonso didn't hesitate an instant in agreeing. As a matter of fact, it was the worst government imaginable. Affirming it that way, so simply, for the first time in so many years, so very many years, and admitting it here, among people he had never met before and whom he would never see again, who were his own son's age, demonstrated to him that in fact he had fervently known it for a long time. An inexplicable image, whose origin he could not imagine, arose in his mind. Saying yes that way was like admitting the existence of a Siamese twin who did not appear in the mirror but who had been there waiting ever since birth for that one moment of light to reveal himself. Yes. The government was exactly how Alvaro Parada had described it.

"And shit is not eternal. No one can convince me that shit is either eternal or irrevocable. Some day . . . My books will come out sooner or later."

It was his wife who intervened, who spoke those words that Don Alfonso had been about to pronounce: "But it would be better if they came out sooner, right?"

The writer smiled. He took his wife's hand. "Of course. No

doubt about it. It would also be better if the government fell. That's the way things are; what can you do?"

Don Alfonso tried to ignore the woman's stare as he pondered what to say next. He felt as though he had been caught red-handed in a wig and makeup.

"I'm going to be completely frank and honest with you, too, sir," he said, energetically. A light smile played at the woman's lips. "You are a man of talent. Bergante knows that, a few other men of less courage than he know it, and I know it . . . The question is whether you also want the general public in this country to know it."

"There's nothing I want more than that," he replied passionately.

"Nothing?" asked his wife. "Nothing?"

"It's what I want most," the writer stated.

"Then it's a question of tactics," Don Alfonso went on. "If you would just lighten up a bit on your political content . . . No, no, wait just a minute, I'm not saying to drop it entirely, just to go a little lighter. After you've had a little publishing success, then, fine, it'll be easier to get works accepted that are . . . let's say, works that are more direct, if you see what I mean . . ."

The writer stood up. He released his wife's hand, as she attempted to stop his next words.

"Carlos is behind this visit! That bandit! It's all clear now. He's tried the same thing before. But he's never gone so far as disguising one of his own friends and making him play a role."

"You're offending me, sir," retorted Don Alfonso, also getting to his feet.

"I really don't care if he sent you or not. I've already told Bergante and I'm telling you now. I refuse to drop even a comma or a semicolon, not one . . . nothing." Seeing that Don Alfonso was going to protest his innocence once more, the writer hastened on: "Forgive my outburst. Caution, prudence, care. Fine. If we've learned to survive, it's because we bite our tongues every day, every minute. Working within the rules of the game. Fine. You don't do any good if you write just to be censored, just to provoke the government or to prove how bad it is . . . It's a problem of limits, that's all."

He stopped, perplexed, trying to find the right words. Don

Alfonso took advantage of the occasion to set down the empty coffee cup that to his surprise was still in his hand.

"Limits?" he asked, because he didn't know what else to say or do, as the silence prolonged itself.

The children stopped playing and the three of them sat down in a row, watching their father.

"Mr. Gacitúa . . . I'm going to explain myself by using something from my novel. Do you remember the scene, near the end, when they're torturing . . . Ernesto, your namesake, the son of José Córdova? Do you remember that part?"

"What? You mean the boy is arrested? I didn't read that far."

"He has to pretend he isn't in the resistance. He presumes those fellows don't know about his real revolutionary activities, as is the case nine times out of ten . . . He has to convince them that he's apolitical, something of a skeptic, with no faith at all. But at the same time, he can't sacrifice his dignity. Do you understand me? He can't lick their boots and pretend that he agrees with them. Those implacable shadows have the power of life and death over him and he must hide everything he knows from them, and that's a lot, if you remember. He's going to lie, deceive, disorient them, but not at the cost of his own human dignity. There's a limit beyond which he knows he cannot go. If he loses what he carries within him, if he sacrifices that wall of fire that he knows is there deep down in his own suffering, then they've really screwed him; they've screwed him even if he doesn't say a word. Because from that moment on he's going to have to lie to himself for the rest of his life in order to endure having lost that part of himself. That's the limit I'm talking about. That's the only thing that interests me. It's why I write, why we're so, well . . . the way you see us here. I'll keep quiet, whatever you want, as long as it doesn't tie me to their truth. And if that means I have to wait a thousand years, then I'll wait a thousand, and if it means never, then never."

"So all of this was for nothing." Don Alfonso heard his own voice pronouncing the words, filtering over that wretched apartment, those children, his wife's tired face.

"Excuse me, Don Ernesto," he said. "But you haven't understood a thing. I refer you to the novel. Remember what happened to José Córdova . . ."

Don Alfonso couldn't help blushing, but, feeling the weight of
the woman's eyes, he did manage to resist scratching his left ear.

"What does happen to José Córdova?" he asked, trying to hide
the tremble in his voice. "I didn't finish reading the manuscript."

"No way, Don Ernesto. You know the golden rule in our profes-
sion. When the book comes out, buy it. You'll find out."

"What if I have to wait a thousand years, as you yourself have
suggested?"

"That depends on you," Mrs. Parada suddenly said.

"Don Alfonso became alarmed. "On me? Why does it depend
on me?"

"It depends on all of us," Alvaro Parada said. "That's what my
wife means. I'm not blaming your firm that doesn't want to risk
publishing it. It depends on it, on me, on you, on every citizen of
this country. Every little effort wears the government down. Maybe
you can read the book in another five hundred years."

"Or next year," his wife added. "Or the day after tomorrow."

"I really must go," said Don Alfonso. "Thank you for the coffee,
madam."

She shook her head, as if she were just waking up from a dream.
She blinked several times, stared at him fixedly and then lowered
her eyes. At that moment Don Alfonso realized that she had come
close to something that she did not want to admit.

Just then the writer added: "Are you sure that we've never met
before, Don Ernesto? I mean, I know we haven't, but your face is
so . . . I don't know . . . so familiar somehow . . ." He didn't finish
his sentence.

"I must go," Don Alfonso quickly repeated. "I've intruded on
your Saturday and that is unforgivable."

"The child will be born at any rate," Parada stated, pointing in
the direction of the table and the typewriter. "It isn't good to delay
it, but everything will happen in its own time."

Don Alfonso tried not to look at the woman's face. He knew
that her eyes continued to avoid him as well. "I'll be in touch with
you when your novel comes out, and see if you're interested in
publishing the second one with our firm."

Don Alfonso extended his hand first to the writer, then to his
wife.

The woman was still watching her children. "Good luck, sir," she said, her voice broken, breathless, as if she were chewing on every word. "Good luck to you and to your family, sir. I wish you well."

"Good luck to all of us," the writer joked, but Don Alfonso did not want to stay another minute, and took his leave. Pushed gently by their mother, the children accompanied him to the ground floor and when he turned to look at the building for the last time, from the end of the alley, they were still watching him from the distance. They waved good-bye, all of them in unison, as if he were some relative who was going away forever, slightly dragging one leg. "Say good-bye to your uncle," she had said. "Say good-bye to Uncle Ernesto."

On Monday, Don Alfonso arrived at the office in mid-morning. Two months earlier he had gotten permission, because he had a dentist appointment. With the floating sensation of unreality that comes with having a tooth pulled, as if he were in a fog, he took the elevator to the floor where his office was.

The first thing he noticed was that the manuscript was missing.

"*Turns?*" mused the secretary. Oh, yes, sir. Carlos Bergante had been by early that morning to pick it up. Did he leave a message? Nothing special. Just thank you and he would call.

Don Alfonso dialed the publisher's number.

"Bergante? Look, what's this business of coming for the manuscript? Didn't I tell you that I was postponing my decision until today?"

Bergante apologized. He hadn't wanted to waste any more of his time. Everything was perfectly clear to both of them. When Don Alfonso, the king of censors, the final word, old eagle eye himself, affirmed that there were problems, the book was condemned to total annihilation. It was no use having talent if you didn't know how to obey the rules of the game . . . It was all right. He would send him another manuscript early next week.

Don Alfonso didn't recognize his own voice. He listened to the words that he was going to say now as though someone else were uttering them, like listening to a voice on a tape and not recognizing it as your own.

"You're wrong, Bergante," that voice was saying. "And just to make you aware of your mistaken opinion, I'm telling you that it is my official judgment that the book should be published."

There was utter silence at the other end of the line.

"You don't usually kid around, Don Alfonso. I hope this isn't the first time."

He answered carefully, choosing each phrase like a newly ripe piece of fruit.

"This is a serious business. You know, Bergante, that one risks his job with every decision."

"Not just his job," Bergante replied. "You risk your neck."

"Exactly," Don Alfonso's voice declared.

"Who is going to authorize the book when it comes out then?" asked the publisher.

"Send it directly to me. I'll see that it goes through."

There was another silence, as though the other man didn't recognize Don Alfonso's voice either.

"Is that a promise?"

"I'm not in the habit of making promises that I do not intend to keep."

"I can't believe you're saying this to me. Not in this country."

"Maybe things are changing," Don Alfonso heard his voice saying into the telephone of the Information Ministry. "Have a good day, Bergante."

Three months later, the printed book reached his desk. Don Alfonso didn't make the least effort to read it. He didn't even open it. He reached for a sheet of paper that said AUTHORIZED UNCONDITIONALLY at the top and signed it without hesitation. He called Bergante at once.

"I'm a man of my word," he said. "The book can be distributed."

Bergante replied that distribution would begin that very afternoon. By tomorrow morning it would be in all the bookstores in the capital. They were also launching a special publicity campaign. Wouldn't he like for him to send him a copy autographed by the author?

"No, thank you," said Don Alfonso. "That isn't necessary. Congratulate the young man for me."

The next day he didn't go to the office. He was awakened late by the insistent ringing of the phone. He let it ring, as if it were just a lullaby, and then he got up to fix a big, Sunday-style breakfast. He opened the windows wide, letting in a pale, late winter sunlight. The phone rang again, but Don Alfonso ignored it.

Later he walked to the bookstore around the corner.

"May I help you?"

"I'm looking for a new book. Maybe you haven't gotten it in yet."

The salesman smiled triumphantly. "I bet I know the book you're looking for. *Turns*. Right?"

Don Alfonso's eyes must have registered his surprise.

"It's just that everyone is buying it," the salesman informed him. "I got twenty copies in last night and I only have two left. Imagine that. Only two. I've never seen such a sudden success. Everybody is asking for it."

"And to what do you attribute such success?" Don Alfonso asked, taking the book that the salesman was offering him, as if he had never seen it before.

"I haven't read it, sir. But I've heard it's scandalous, really scandalous. It must be, the way people are buying it up."

"Oh, really? That bad, huh?"

"I couldn't say, sir. I kept a copy for myself. I already sent it home. You never know in a case like this. They say it's a strong attack on the government, sir. No one can understand how it was ever authorized."

"Fine," said Don Alfonso. "You'd better give me another copy then. I'll take your last two copies."

"Very wise, sir," said the salesman. "The case may go to court at any moment and the judge demand that the entire edition be confiscated. But the harm's already done . . . Would you like them gift-wrapped?"

"No, thank you. That's fine."

As he left the shop, Don Alfonso saw a police van, the assault division, approaching at great speed. He went on calmly walking toward his house, refusing to turn around when he heard the screech of brakes, the slamming of doors, and the footsteps of police agents jumping from the van and entering the bookstore.

The phone was ringing again. This time Don Alfonso answered.

"Don Alfonso." His secretary's voice was excited. "The Director wants to see you. The Minister himself has been here. Today of all days when you didn't come in to work. The Director wants to talk to you."

"Tell him I won't be in at all today."

"Wait. Just a moment while I connect you with the Director."

This time Don Alfonso was not surprised at his own voice. He recognized every word he was about to say.

"I can't talk to him," said Don Alfonso. "I have things to do. Tell him I'm going to be busy all day."

Not waiting for a reply, he hung up. Then he took the receiver off the hook, so he couldn't be interrupted again.

Very calmly, he took one of the two books and with his famous black ballpoint pen he wrote an inscription on the cover, just under the author's name, for his son. He wrapped it as a gift, very methodically, and went to leave it on the bed, so that his son would see it when he came in that night. Later, he changed his mind and stuck it under the pillow.

Only then did he go and sit down in his favorite armchair in front of the large window. If a car braked or stopped, if somebody knocked on the door, if they came for a visit, he would see everything from that privileged spot.

He felt himself driven by a sudden haste.

He opened the book and, knowing that he no longer needed his eyes to look at the street again, he set about reading once and for all what Don José Córdova's decision had finally been.

MY HOUSE IS ON FIRE

"Lady bug, lady bug,
Fly away home.
Your house is on fire.
Your children will burn."

Mother Goose

"Listen," she says, "Do you think it's the enemy? Listen."

It's better not to answer her. If it is the enemy, there's no time to lose talking. Both of us heard the noise of the car and that's enough: first it stopped, braked with a screech, and now it must be there, parked in front by the sidewalk, the motor running. Let's just hide and leave the questions for later.

"Nobody can see us; nobody can see us," she sings. "Here in our pretty little house, nobody can see us."

Don't I wish. I bring the chair closer, pushing it gently with my legs. I take the corner of the blanket that she offers me, and tying it to mine, I attach both of them firmly to the legs of the chair, pulling them as tight as a wind-furled sail. Now we can go into our house. She gets down on her knees and crawls in; I follow after taking a quick look around; there's just enough room for two in here. I hope she understands—that's the main thing. We have to watch our voices, whisper. No cries. No temper tantrums.

As usual, she ignores me. "Okay," she says, sighing with satisfaction. "Safe and sound. Now it's your turn to choose a game."

It's easier for me if she thinks it's just a game, if she doesn't suspect that it's a real war, that this time it's really serious. She's going to pretend to be the mother and I'm going to be the father, and we're going to get ready for the enemy's arrival. We're going to go over everything and talk about it the way they did last night, when they thought we were asleep, okay?

She lifts a fold of the blanket like a window to look outside. "I just don't remember," she says. "Since I'm the mother, I'd better cook something for you and the kids. Hey, do you want me to make something special? I'm a really good cook."

What kind of mother is gonna start cooking now? Didn't she hear the car, the enemy's car? Doesn't she know that they always pick rainy days to come? Maybe they're coming for me, the father, and she can't be cooking, she has to do other things, if that happens. Remember what Mama said.

"Oh," she answers, forming her words with surprising energy. "I know what I have to do. The mother has to tell somebody. I tell . . . I tell . . ."

Leandro. I ask her to repeat the name. Let's see if you remember it the next time. Le-an-dro.

"Leandro. I tell Leandro," she says. And then adds, "Hey, do you know Leandro?"

Neither of us knows Leandro. She doesn't; I don't. Juan knows, and he's told me and made me promise not to spill the beans. It's a big secret. Because, well, Leandro's the Party contact. If I keep the secret, then someday Juancho's going to introduce me to Leandro and even explain about the Party, so I'm not going to tell her anything. Women can't keep secrets; that's what Juancho said; silence is golden. I'll just say that Leandro's a guy we don't know, a really great guy, bright as the sun, big as a whale and generous as a garden. Really a fantastically fantastic guy.

"When my uncle Leandro comes," she says, "he's gonna bring me lots of presents, 'cause he really loves me."

Just then one of the blankets falls down—the one she tied, naturally; it had to be that one. There's a big hole in the roof, the size of a clown's mouth. Now we really have to hurry and work together to get the house fixed, before the enemy can take advantage . . . Go bring me some of Papa's books, please, the really big ones . . . Of course she takes forever, dilly-dallying around, and if the enemy decides to attack now, we're really done for. But when she gets back she seems like such a baby and is smiling and I don't say anything. What for?

"Hey," she says, still not handing me the books—she must think we have all day. "Somebody got out of that car."

I decide to pretend indifference to keep from upsetting her. Which car?

"The enemy's. I looked through the window, you know. I'm a really good spy."

And what if they saw her? What'll happen? If they saw her, what then? She'd better just hand me the books.

She gets in the house as calm as you please, doesn't even answer my question, and from there, while I secure the blankets with books, she starts to hum a little song. I finish putting the books in their place and then I crawl in. I brush off my knees carefully and ask her if she thinks the enemy saw her. What if they decided to cart her off, too? Her, the mother?

She stops humming then, and a cloud comes over her little eyes and she shakes her head.

"That'll never happen," she says. "We're really hidden good."

Pretty little nitwit, of course not. No need to worry so much. Besides, Mama said last night that Juancho knows what he has to do till she gets back. I'm sure they'll let Mama go soon. That's what Papa said.

"They're never going to take our mommy," she insists, raising her voice. "We'll bring her to our little house and they'll never find her."

Okay, okay, but just shut up for now; it's just a game; we're playing, that's all.

"I'm tired of this game," she says. "You always pick games that scare me."

How come I never get scared? Not even when Papa and Mama started talking about us. Not even then.

"About us?" she asks.

Doesn't she remember what Papa and Mama said last night?

"No," she answers, smiling like a dummy. "I fell asleep."

Mama asked about us. What if they decided to take the children with them too, if they decided to take us? She'd never asked that before. She said it so soft and whispery that I could hardly hear her.

"But nobody can find us, right?" she asks.

"No way."

She raises both hands victoriously.

"We're really hiding good," she says, happy.

Then Papa started to fuss with her. She shouldn't ask stupid questions. He talked so loud and so mad that Mama came in to see us. She thought he'd awakened us with all the noise. Mama didn't know I wasn't sleeping. I shut my eyes real tight, so she wouldn't find out. I felt her lips on my cheek; they stayed there a long time, warm and close; the kiss just seemed to last forever, then she went over to the other bed. She must have stayed there a long time, just looking at us; for a minute I thought she'd found us out. But time passed and I just stayed there behind my eyes, curled up under the sheet, still listening to the echo of her voice, asking Papa in a loud whisper, what if they take the children, then what, while she watched us sleep, and then I heard her footsteps in the hall, going away, back to where Papa was.

"And then what did they say?" she asked. "What did they say about me?"

Shut up. Hear that? That noise?

"What noise?" she says.

The door. Did she hear that? Somebody knocking at the door.

"My uncle Leandro," she announces, almost clapping. "Let's open the door. Come on, Pablito."

Don't even move. What's the matter with her? Let me listen. Yeah. It sounds like the one who went to open the door was Papa.

"Are they coming to look for us?" she asks. "If it's not Uncle Leandro, do you think it could be the enemy? Hey, listen, do you think . . ."

How does she expect me to find out anything if she keeps on jabbering? She should just pay attention, like me. That's Papa's voice, isn't it? Now another man's answering. I really don't recognize that voice at all. I don't remember it.

"Now what are they doing?"

They must have come in the house. Yeah. One of them closed the door. Slammed it like he was mad. Okay, now, for Pete's sake, it's time for this baby bird to keep quiet. We're gonna pretend we're a couple of little mice, and we've forgotten how to talk.

"Then I'm gonna look through this little hole," she says. "I'm a spy mouse."

I tell her to be still. Not to touch anything.

"I'm bored," she says. "Let me look through the hole. Don't be mean, Pablito."

Just tell me one thing. One little thing. Is she the mother or not? Yes or no?

"Yes," she answers. "Of course I'm the mother."

Then she has to do what I say, right, because I'm the father. So she should stay here, protecting the house, and just be quiet, not say a word, because if they catch us it's gonna be her fault and nobody else's.

She puts her mouth to my ear and whispers really slowly, tickling me with her breath. It's a soft, warm breath, like a rabbit's; something tender runs up my back. I remember Mama's kiss last night and suddenly I feel like giving a big hug to this little sister of mine who's so small and defenseless. "Listen, Papa," that voice whispers, "do you think they're coming to look for us?"

Frankly, I think they are; the situation's getting dangerous. But how can I explain that to the little lamb? She'd probably start to cry, go to pieces on me right now, when it's really important to have nerves of steel. Being the father, I'll just have to tell her the same thing Papa said last night. They wouldn't dare take the kids. Sure, they're fascists, but even they wouldn't go that far.

"They're scared of us," she says, satisfied.

If she doesn't be quiet, they're sure to catch us, and that's the gospel truth. Listen, they're really close, in the other room.

We stay like that awhile; so quiet it seems like a miracle, one of those catacombs that Juan used to talk about: silent, alone with our own breathing, hidden far from the world. I take her fingers and put them on her lips, and she smiles at me. From the next room we can hear the voices of several men, two, three, maybe even more. Now's the time to keep cool and to be absolutely still. As if they weren't there.

"Since I'm the mother . . ." Her words resound suddenly, almost like a gunshot; in that perfect silence her voice expodes like the cry of some wild bird; you can probably hear it everywhere in the house; it takes me by surprise. "Shall I tell 'em to go away?"

Uselessly, I put my finger to my lips. Uselessly, because they've already heard her. No doubt. Someone is slowly opening the door of the room where we are, you can just hear the hinges squeak a little and someone coming in with a heavy step; somebody turns on the light and it bursts through the blanket like the big white eye of a crazy man; now they're coming. They're the ones who've come.

My finger freezes on my lips. "Listen," she insists—I can't believe it, pulling at my shirt besides—"they have to obey me, don't they? If I'm the mother?"

The only thing left for me to do is to signal for her to hide her head in her arms, to see if that'll keep her quiet. If she was really the mother, then she'd show it by being quiet, by holding her tongue, just like last night, when Papa demanded it, when he told her that it was no use talking about these things, that she should just stop that kind of talk once and for all, that we're ready for any eventuality. I waited there in the darkness; she had already fallen asleep, so she didn't bother anybody; Mama had gone back to join Papa. I waited for them to go on talking, but they didn't say anything, not a word. I got up really quiet and went out into the hall to hear them better, and I moved closer, but keeping in the shadows, the light was still on in the bedroom, but they didn't say another word, it was as if the silence had swallowed them, neither he nor she, Mama nor Papa; they were there looking at each other, sitting facing each other but not saying a word, not opening their mouths.

Fortunately my sister starts to pay attention to me now; at least she hides her head in her arms. That way she won't be afraid; she won't be able to see the shadow up there, cold and distant, up there above the blankets, two shadows, trying to listen. There are at least two men there, at least two, outside our house, and neither of them says a word. They're waiting for us to make a mistake. They've been watching us for days, getting closer, the evidence is in that they're about to pounce. But they're not gonna get us. We'll be still, as if we're lost or sleeping or dead; the enemy will have to go away empty-handed.

"They won't be able to find us," she says, putting one hand over her mouth to hold in a burst of nervous laughter. "We're too well hidden."

What's the use in telling the dummy to keep quiet? Why even talk to her? It's hopeless. Now I can see the ceiling opening up, pulled back by enormous hands, and the blankets fall off like a house of cards and the light penetrates our hideaway sharper and quicker than a sword stroke, and the two shadows are two men out there, up there, and they're staring at us without saying anything. They caught us and it's all her fault, all because of that idiot. It's the last time I'll play with her, cross my heart and hope to die, the last time.

The brutal violence of the light makes me blink, and then I recognize Papa. Lucky that one of the men is Papa. But there's somebody else beside him, a big, dark guy, taller and heavier than Papa, with his coat still on and dripping with rain, somebody I've never seen before, somebody I don't know, somebody who's examining us in our own house as if he had X-ray vision.

She still doesn't see him, because she still has her thick head hidden under her arms, just like an ostrich. There, on her knees, with her rear end in the air, you can just see the edge of her panties below her skirt. The next time I'll have to muzzle this woman, that's what I'll have to do.

"Go away," the fresh little thing orders, as though nothing had happened and we weren't at their mercy. "We're not here. We're someplace else."

He laughs, laughs with that same voice that came from the next room and that I can't remember ever hearing before. He laughs real loud.

"So you're not here, are you?" he says. "Nobody's here?"

Papa, on the other hand, is not laughing. He looks at us sternly and moves one of the chairs, which makes the rest of our house fall down and the blankets are spread around as if there'd been an earthquake or some terrible cyclone.

"Come on out, kids," says Papa, upset, and with his mind on other things. "Come out right now."

When she hears Papa's voice, then she finally realizes they've caught us, so she stands up and rubs her eyes like somebody who's really sleepy and then looks first at Papa and then at the other man.

"I don't know you," she finally says. "But you're a new uncle . . ." She tilts her head to one side, studying him, like a sparrow about ready to take off, and then adds, "What's your name anyway?"

It's too late now. We're surrounded. There's no way to tell her what she should do or say. She's forgotten all the instructions; all the preparations were for nothing. How can I make her understand that it's not an uncle at all, that this time it's more serious, that our whole family's in danger?

"What's my name?" he asks, with a half-smile that's not really disagreeable, in fact it's surprisingly friendly. "I bet you can't guess."

Papa is about to interrupt, but she's faster and cuts him off. Not even Papa can save us now. "Leandro!" screams the idiot. "I bet you're my uncle Leandro!"

The man exchanges a glance with Papa, watches him a moment, and picking up one of the big books that are still on the chair, he turns it over to read the title.

"You're absolutely right," he says slowly, after a pause. "That's what they call me—Leandro . . . But I don't know how you guessed. It's supposed to be a secret."

"We're really smart," she says, as talkative as ever, as trusting as ever, unable to recognize the enemy when he's standing right in front of her eyes, confusing the enemy with a friend, the kid's gonna be like this till the day she dies. "Look, Uncle Leandro, see how well we were hiding. I bet it was really hard for you to find us, wasn't it?"

"Really, really hard," the man says, turning the book over and over, opening and closing it. "It took months."

Now Papa picks her up in his arms and presses her against him, to see if that'll keep her quiet. I realize that he still has one arm free, hanging at his side. I go up beside him and with my ten fingers, with my two palms, with my two strong arms, like angels made out of dirt, I grab that enormous hand of his, I hold on to it real tight, with rage, with trust, like I was never going to let it go, like I was holding on to a pier before saying good-bye and leaving on a long trip.

Then the man turns his attention to me.

"And what about this little man? What's the matter with him?" he asks. "Are you afraid to open your mouth? Or did the cat get your tongue?"

I could tell him that the cat didn't get my tongue, that I'm my father's son and that the men in this family are never afraid. But it's better not to answer. The man stands there watching me, waiting for me to say something, anything, and I stay as quiet as ever, they won't get a word out of me. Let him keep on asking my sister; she's the one that spills the beans. But I can't prevent the silence from becoming very heavy, irritating and unbearable. All we can hear is the persistent sound of the rain beating on the roof and wind rustling the wet leaves of the trees along the street. Everybody's looking at me, waiting for some sign that I'm not a deafmute, that I'm not a hopeless imbecile.

Outside the room there are footsteps, running footsteps, and we all turn around toward the door, which opens just at that moment and Juan comes in; thank God it's Juancho, Juancho who always knows what to do. He's coming from school, water is running down his face and he still has his bookbag in his hand. He stands behind me right away, as though he knew I needed him. I feel comforted, protected, by Juancho's formidable presence, his warmth, like a bonfire behind me. Together, Juancho, Papa and me can face the whole world, the fiercest monsters in the whole world. He drops his bookbag and whispers in my ear. His words are wet and sound like the buzzing of a bumblebee as it flies against the window. They're so low and fast and confused that I can't even understand what he's saying, nobody could, something about secrets and promises and other things.

Papa chooses that moment to try to get away, that very moment. I can feel the way his fingers are trying to pull away, naturally he needs both hands to put her down, so he'll be completely free. But I hold on tight, I won't let go; I wouldn't let go of Papa's big, warm paw for anything in the world. It's beating there like my second heart and I hold on to him as if he were the last tree in the yard and I was his favorite nest.

Suddenly, it's the man who breaks the silence, like someone who throws a football into a window and breaks it to smithereens. It's the man who speaks again and incredibly he is speaking to my brother.

"Hey, Juancho," he says. "It looks like you've trained this little guy well. I still haven't been able to pull a single word out of him. He's as tight as a clam."

I feel Juancho pushing me a little, but I don't budge; nobody can move me an inch if I don't want to move. Then in the middle of that silence that once again begins to spread out like something dark and full of rain, she opens up beside me, like a sun-drenched terrace; she's the one who knows what to do; she's the one who answers for me.

"The thing is," she says, stepping forward, "nobody has introduced you. That's the reason. Uncle Leandro, I want you to meet my brother. His name's Pablito. He's a little shy, but you can trust him. Pablito, this is our uncle Leandro."

He returns the book to the chair and looks at me.

"So you're the famous Pablito," he says. "They've told me a lot about you. They say you're just like your old man, a real chip off the old block. A real man. Is that right?"

I wait a few more impossible seconds and weigh his glance, the way his eyes could give and receive an answer, the way his shoulders rest beneath the coat, the generous strength of his hands, the calm in that smile which is starting to grow and hide itself in his lips. I'd like to remain anchored to Papa's hand; I really wish there were just the two of us, alone, or if not the two of us, at least just the family, and that we were far away from here, maybe out on a playground or across the sea or behind some mountain, under a different sky. But here is where we are, where I am, and now my fingers must be the ones that are struggling to break free and now nobody has to push me forward. My hands are free and I close my eyes a moment, like putting a roof over them, and then I open them, and I'm still here, as alone as a balloon in front of this grown man that I never saw before and don't know. That I don't know.

"Come on, Pablito," I hear Papa's voice saying, "don't be rude, say hello to our friend . . . and, listen, María Victoria, be careful. Maybe the next time it won't be a friend. You have to pay attention."

"But I know that, Papito," she says, smiling. "I always recognize our friends. Anybody can tell."

Anybody can tell, Papa? Anybody?

"Hello, Leandro," said Pablo, trying to sound like a grown-up.

CROSSINGS

The names of those generals and commandants now have been given to avenues and plazas, their oil portraits hang in museums and mansions, students recite their deeds with veneration, and the horses they once mounted are now equestrian statues at the intersections of boulevards. He, on the other hand, had never been given so much as a mention in a footnote or a corner in the great paintings of the period. Not even a scrawny alley, not a fragment of a speech, not even words carved on an unknown tombstone. One might ask if he perhaps knew that's the way things would be. Perhaps he did; perhaps he didn't. The only thing of which we can be sure is that, for him, such problems didn't exist; they didn't have the least importance; he never asked such a question. He was concerned with other things.

Bruno Santelices (pseudonym),
"Prologue" to *The People's New History
of the Wars of Independence*

"The flight is not delayed," the young woman behind the information desk announces to me, so everything is as scheduled, only forty minutes before the plane from Buenos Aires lands, the one on which you're supposed to arrive.

Imagining you on board is not difficult. As usual you will be occupying an aisle seat; you've explained to Arturo that you prefer not to feel like a sardine, your own cage is enough. Perhaps at this very moment you are listening to the excited voice of some child—why shouldn't there be one seated nearby, probably in your own row?—who is pointing out the window, insisting that his father look at the panorama. And simultaneously the intrusion of the pilot, who announces that on your right, ladies and gentlemen, is Mt. Aconcagua, with its well-known six thousand and more meters above sea level, it hasn't grown one gray centimeter since your last trip, the Queen of the Andes, the peak of the Americas, and no doubt the passengers' excited murmurs will invade you, a tidal wave of exclamations and whispers, of pointing fingers and exploding flashbulbs, and for one relieved moment, it's as though the humming of the motors had been abolished.

Even though you should, even though it would help you to pass the time, somehow you can't bring yourself to adopt the role of tourist, pull out the Fushica that's resting in the bag lying open at your feet along with your travel documents, some untouched books and an immense doll with blue eyes, long lashes and golden hair that would be a fine gift for a daughter, if you had one. But you don't reach for your camera, you won't look for it. You touch your seatbelt. Fortunately there are only forty minutes left.

At this point it doesn't matter how many times you've made the crossing. You now feel suffocated by that sensation that started earlier, when you'd hardly stepped through the plane door, a sensation you had managed to overcome then and that you did not want to define, but that now, with those silent mountains below you, crossing the vague border of what must be Chile, is gradually assuming a rather clear name: it's called fear, a fear which you can later confess with one of your mocking and distant smiles, but which is nonetheless taking possession of you, creeping up your arms to your throat from hands that grow damper and damper, and are now, despite what your brain orders, downright wet with sweat. How easy it is to imagine the way in which you sense the acceleration of your own body, something weak and fluttering that could betray you, something that is undermining you from inside, the sudden and overwhelming need to go to the bathroom, to go through the lavatory door and find yourself in your own house just waking up from a nightmare, or in some other time, attached to some other spinal column; how easy it is to imagine your all-pervading need to parachute out of there as soon as the mountain range looms in the distance.

"Fear is natural," Arturo once told you when, inevitably, your conversation turned to that topic, too; he said it when you came back from your first trip. "I wouldn't trust anybody who wasn't afraid."

"Thanks," you said.

"You're welcome," said Arturo. And then added quickly: "As far as fear goes, you know, if I were you, I wouldn't pretend it's not there. Being ashamed of something that's real is no good. I'd look it right in the eye. That's the best way to handle it. Treat it like an old friend, as they say."

You tried to minimize the whole thing, pretending it was a joke. "The thing is I don't like its face. It's ugly as hell."

Arturo is not one of those people who try to persuade others with speeches and moralizing. He spreads calm just by being there, by the way he goes about offering you a cup of coffee when the world is falling in on you, by the way he lights a cigarette, ever so carefully, and then lets the match go out by itself in the ashtray, while he lovingly admires the first puff of smoke, relishing it, even when you know he has a thousand things on his mind; by that open and alert serenity with which he sits back and absorbs your every word, by all the little things, all of them.

"So what did you say in response?" I offhandedly asked Arturo later, when he was talking the matter over with me, measuring my own reactions, inviting me to get involved in the whole thing, I, who never talk about anything personal and am not used to confidences.

"I said it's like the face of the enemy," Arturo answered, cautiously, as he sought out my eyes. " 'If you never look at his photograph,' I said, 'you'll never be able to recognize him in time, and then he might take you by surprise around any street corner, you know.' "

I didn't say anything, but, according to Arturo, you did; you had an answer on the tip of your tongue.

"Easy with the metaphors," you replied. "You can't live by pulling out the enemy's picture from the family album every other minute to look at it, either. Right?"

"Right," Arturo agreed, just as I would have done. "If you devote too much time to it, the fear will end up growing so big it'll paralyze you; it'll devour you. I know people who've fallen in love with their own fear."

So I didn't say anything, but you: "That would be like falling in love with the enemy."

"What I can offer you," Arturo smiled, "are some mental exercises; you discipline your mind by shifting attention to other things."

"Thanks," you said.

" 'It's nothing at all,' I said," Arturo explained to me, without giving any details on the type of exercises he had prescribed, perhaps waiting for some question from me, or an opinion, something. But I didn't say anything.

You thought the second trip would be different, that after having talked things over with Arturo, your mood would change. But as usual, all the advice had been of little value. There was the same old fear, on the flight's itinerary, as if the pilot could have announced it along with the speed of the plane and the northeast winds we'd be hitting in just a few minutes, fasten your seatbelts, prepare for sudden loss of altitude, the fear rising in you, slow and sinuous as the hills which are becoming more and more prominent on the Mendoza side, until all of a sudden, when the first gigantic, rocky peaks appear stabbing the sky, twisted by millions of years of volcanic eruptions, the fear is there, too, like some demon arriving for a date, right on time.

So the only thing left for you to do then, as now, was to think of me; you try to imagine my presence, waiting for you in Pudahuel, thanking the lady at the LAN-Chile desk for her helpful information, only forty minutes to go. You have to concentrate on me, bring me to life in your imagination, focus my figure in your memory and anchor yourself to it, think of me right now walking toward the restroom with slow but firm steps, listening for the sound of the loudspeakers, pushing the door and deciding to go in, even though I don't need to.

For one moment you even imagine yourself in the toilet of the Boeing; you can almost feel the refreshing touch of a paper towel soaked in water, with a sprinkling of eau de cologne, your own image suddenly and surprisingly present in the mirror, the chestnut hair, the dark, shining eyes that don't reflect the slightest hint of fear, that body that seems so far away and so confident, with no suggestion of what an excessively fertile sensibility is putting you through every step of the way. But it's best not to move, not to risk the certainty of the emptiness beneath your feet, just answer the stewardess who is asking if you need anything: thank you; everything is wonderful, but, as a matter of fact, a shot of whiskey would be nice; then the two dollars, in coins, counting them out, then watching how the ice falls into the clear, plastic glass, yes, no water, thank you, that's fine, even though afterward you don't touch it, don't even lift it to your lips; it's there near you like a friend who understands everything and is able to calm you down. Perhaps at that very moment, by one of those strange coincidences, I am also walking into the bar, after cleaning my glasses and drying my hands. From the airport's second story one can see the runway, the coming and going of the usual military trucks. It's only natural for me to order a drink, too, just to pass the time, to hurry the plane along and make it land at last, trusting that you're on board; one never knows. But you must suppose that I really do drink it, without looking at the man beside me who is impatiently demanding a Tom Collins, first just sipping at it and then, as my thirst grows, really guzzling it; wanting to save something for later while the swallows clutch at my throat and refuse to let go, and then gazing at the blatantly blue sky there beyond the mountains where I can't catch even a glimpse of you, not even a helicopter or a bird, and then gulping down the last drop, just at the moment when they bring the Tom Collins to the man beside me, and digging my hands deep into my pockets and figuring that yes, we can indulge in the luxury of one more gin, straight up.

It's now, as the moments stretch out and become impossibly sticky, now that I begin to look around—a stabilizing exercise— and find myself staring at a woman dressed entirely in black, so shabbily dressed that she stands out like an eyesore in Pudahuel among so many tourists and travelers, accompanied by two small children and showing visible signs of recent tears. Who knows what she's doing there in the airport, maybe picking up a casket arriving from overseas, saying good-bye to a relative who's being deported. Now is the moment to take an interest in other people's fortunes in order to keep from looking at your own life, at the uncertainty of your immediate future, to take note of the fact that about fifteen paces behind that woman a bulk of a man is walking, that the man stops, indecisive, when the woman goes into the restroom, and that now he moves toward the bar and, entering, sits down near me, beside the man who ordered the Tom Collins; it's now that up there you would also have to notice the people around you, concentrating, for example, on the conversation between the child and his father, the ones in your own row. It occurs to me that the father may have promised the child a story, something for when the descent begins. Maybe the child has asked for a tale about the mountains and the father hesitates, clears his throat, and finally gives in.

So you listen because you don't have anything better to do, and, as for me, I can imagine the scene for myself, as if it were my own son there beside the window, as if I were telling him a bedtime story, the way I would if he were not out there, in another country, with his mother. It's easy to conjure up the characters, the airplane, both easy and necessary to fill this exasperatingly slow period of time with something besides that woman who never seems to come out of the restroom and the man who orders nothing in the bar and who has not taken his eyes off that door marked WOMEN, easy to imagine that I could be the one sitting there beside you and talking instead of being here, nursing this glass of gin, straight up, as if it were some kind of precious stone, drop by drop, because I don't have a single cent for another drink and I don't want one anyway, while you shut your eyes and try not to miss even one syllable of the story, and what better way is there to kill your minutes and mine than with a story about the mountains, about a muleteer who lived a hundred fifty years ago, one of those strange stories Arturo likes to tell, one of his mental exercises perhaps, a story to which we now listen along with the child while the captain is announcing that the descent to the central valley has begun and that in approximately twenty minutes we will land at Pudahuel International Airport, where you hope, even though you're not sure, that I will be waiting for you, as I always have been, your faithful Pedro, just outside Customs reading a newspaper.

"Crossing the mountains was dangerous back then," I imagine the voice of the man beside you saying, a voice that I conceive of as like Arturo's and perhaps like my own. "But the mountains themselves were not exactly the dangerous part. Because the mountains could do the muleteer no harm. He knew every little pass; he'd explored them with his own father from the time he was a child."

It's not hard to sketch in the child's face; the child, who must be asking if they didn't have any airplanes in those days. And the father answers that no, there weren't any airplanes, or even any trains, or cars; you had to make the crossing on foot or mule. Of course that muleteer had made the crossing thousands of times and under every imaginable condition: the snows of winter and the dust storms of summer. And the muleteer was never late for a meeting.

And now, if I were that father, I would take the child's hand in my own and I would examine the seatbelt, to see if it was fastened securely, while the pilot was reminding the passengers that the NO SMOKING signs had come on, that they should kindly extinguish all cigarettes, and just at that moment you're overwhelmed by the urgent need to smoke, even if it's just one more drag, and the absurd idea of a condemned man being denied his last cigarette crosses your mind, the idea that this is a descent into death, but to erase that thought you need only remember the muleteer who, according to the voice beside you, never arrived late for a meeting.

Of course not. He always appeared at the agreed-upon hour, serene and imperturbable. Not even the condors knew the Andes so well. He knew the glaciers, the hidden waterfalls to quench his thirst, all the tricks of the fogs, and how to predict the rain before it fell. Legends were spun about him as the men who would cross the mountains and liberate Chile gathered around the bonfires. They said, for example, that months ahead of time he had been leaving wood and dried foodstuffs in caves and other refuges; even if it wasn't for his own use, someone would need it. They said there was always a woman waiting for him at the other end.

The plane trembles slightly in the air, shaken by a gust of wind, then it turns, banks and begins the descent. A violent burst of sunlight brightens the wing and then disappears. If you felt like it and opened your eyes, you could see the city of Santiago down below, immersed and gagging in its own smog.

No, it really isn't so hard for me to pass the time after all and to participate in the descent myself, anticipating what the father will probably say next, the child's absorbed expression, your own head, cast back, breathing deeply the good oxygen that is abundantly flowing from above your seat. Now that you can't smoke, you'll have to imagine me doing it for the two of us; I stare at the cigarette before lighting it, as if it were some kind of freak. I follow the first whiff of smoke as it drifts up and my eyes go beyond it, to the sky above, looking for that airplane, only sixteen minutes more, according to the schedule, and when my glance falls back to earth, the woman in black is passing the bar, with her two kids by the hand. She reaches the stairway that goes up to the reception area. That man has gone into motion like some kind of robot or puppet and he reaches the stairway and stops there, watching her with his hand on the stair rail. All of a sudden, without my realizing exactly how it happens, another man joins him. It's the same guy who was sitting beside me, the one who ordered and drank the Tom Collins. One of them says something to the other; they wait a short time in silence; now both of them descend the stairs, carefully, as if their feet hurt.

"But it wasn't the gales that threatened the muleteer," the father would have to be explaining by now. And he would ask the child if he knew what could harm the muleteer, what was the only thing he needed to fear, and no, it wasn't the pumas, or the earthquakes or the floods. He asks the child if he can guess what, or who, could harm the muleteer.

"I don't know," says the child.

I put out the cigarette, look at my watch, ask the bartender for my check. It's as though I were up there myself, answering that question, as if Pedro were beside his own son at night before he goes to sleep, comforting him after a nightmare, bringing him a glass of water, bringing him up, answering:

"Men, son. Men could harm him. That's who."

"Men?" You listen; I listen; we both hear the voice of the child who doesn't understand, who certainly can't understand that there are refinements in pain. How do you make him understand, without terrorizing him, without destroying his innocence, that there are places darker than prisons, things harder and sharper than bullets, something far worse than a noose around the neck? How do you make the child stronger, prepare him for life, take away his ignorance, and yet not overwhelm his spirit with problems for which he is not ready? How do you answer when he poses the question that he shouldn't ask, the one he shouldn't ask but deserves to have answered? How do you explain to the kid that the muleteer didn't want to imagine the answer; that it was better to erase the whole matter, not to think about what could happen to him, if, instead of Miguel or Fernando, or Manuel Rodríguez, the one waiting for him at the end of the road were someone else; there were others, men loyal to the king of Spain, the soldiers of Captain San Bruno, who wanted to capture him.

Just now LAN-Chile announces, through a female voice over the loudspeaker, the approaching arrival of flight 112 from Buenos Aires, Montevideo and Rio de Janeiro. I pay for my gins and decide to go out to the Pudahuel terrace, not to go down to the reception area yet, not to have to watch the black figure of that woman, the kids clutching her skirts, the two men, maybe three men by now, watching her from afar or perhaps from closeup with their referees' eyes. The terrace is full to overflowing with splendidly dressed people who are waiting, a regular hullabaloo of voices from children who hang on the railing and scream every time a plane takes off, shouting *Ciao!* to invisible passengers and from others who run around like little devils in a never-ending game of hide-and-seek, slipping in and out between the legs of adults, caught up in other, presumably more important games. And up there one really can see a plane descending, with lingering grace, the plane on which you are probably arriving, on which you have scarcely noticed the rasping drop of the landing wheels. The story of the muleteer is following its course, and closing your eyes again, you lift the glass of whiskey to your lips and you feel on your tongue the bitterness of the liquid, a bit diluted by the ice. You could swear that for one moment you manage to enjoy that state in which nothing depends on you, in which everything is in the hands of other forces, in which your will no longer counts for anything, the cards have already fallen.

You can't be sure that I'm down here; perhaps you imagine my presence in the shadows, watching for that moment when the plane finally makes contact with Chilean soil and you can barely feel the little bump of your own landing. Everything is so gentle that it's impossible to realize that you're still moving at three hundred kilometers per hour and that the mountains are now where they ought to be, there behind you and above you, and that this roar is the engines that are reversing and you can no longer doubt that Pedro will be there waiting for you in that gray building that is Pudahuel lying just ahead. Pedro who, after following the jet's clean landing with his eyes, decides to amble down the stairs that lead to the reception area. Pedro who looks at his watch, calculating the amount of time you'll spend in Immigration, International Police, Customs. Down here the woman in black can no longer be seen anywhere; what can be seen, beside a travel insurance office, is a pair of lovers, kissing and hugging each other as if they were stars on a movie screen, and not two devastated bodies in the middle of Pudahuel Airport, surrendering to each other with abandon and passion, clutching each other's shoulders and hips right there in public, not giving a damn about anything or anybody. It's not clear whether it is she or he who is leaving, their bellies pressed against each other like two boxers in an obscene clinch, like statues, stripped naked and trembling. Her purse slides to the floor and its contents spill out between their feet and neither of them pays any attention; they go on trying to penetrate each other and to merge, as if by allowing one milimeter of traitorous air between their two bodies now, they would lose the right to return and to embrace again. I behold the scene not knowing what to do with

my eyes, where to put them, how to go on watching so much pain
so close up. I can't decide whether to keep still, held by an all-
powerful curiosity, or to turn away and look in another direction
and then, for sure, to see those two men in a corner of the room,
near the passenger exit, the two men who are talking and smoking
and watching that pair of lovers with the same eyes with which
they had watched the woman dressed in black a few moments
earlier.

But you suspect none of this, as the plane rolls on; you of course
have more interest in hearing the story of the muleteer, which is
drawing to a close with the slow pace of all stories told while sitting
on the edge of a child's bed, or around a campfire before the nightly
changing of the guard, or after getting home from school when
there are matters that aren't understood, or at those moments when
planes are landing and trains are arriving and nerves have to be
calmed down and fears removed and eyes have to be pulled away
from a pair of bodies driven by a lonely and unending gale of love;
to cease remembering a rouge, a handkerchief, some keys, lying
at your feet; to concentrate on finding a good seat right in front
of the passenger ramp; to listen to a voice that could be that of
the child's father who is saying that San Bruno would have given
anything to capture that muleteer, to get the valuable information
that only he had. Anybody would have bet that modest little man
could not possibly know anything special. But he was a messenger;
he carried letters that San Martín himself entrusted to him. And
then the muleteer waited for the reply the people in Chile would
give and returned to Mendoza where the Liberating Army was
being formed. And San Bruno was looking for him; he knew neither his face nor his name, but he was on the lookout for him
through his spies, agents and informers. Because the muleteer
knew other things, besides how to deliver letters. The General
talked about everything in his presence. They fixed dates, discussed
hiding places and alternative plans, wrote proclamations which the
muleteer could not read, pronounced French or British names,
repeated or critiqued strategies. The muleteer attended these secret conclaves without uttering a word, calm, unruffled, showing
no emotion, only patience. One month later he would be back.

"What was the muleteer's name, Papa?" I don't know anymore

who asks that question, whether it is the imaginary child on the plane, my own son, or somebody else.

Neither do you; you realize that the motors have stopped, that the pilot is thanking the passengers for having flown LAN-Chile and saying in Spanish that the temperature in Santiago is twenty-five degrees centigrade in the shade; it is four o'clock in the afternoon local time; we hope to have you aboard again sometime; and now the same thing is being repeated in English; you pay less and less attention; you wait, as I do, for the father's answer, the muleteer's name.

"I don't know any more than San Bruno," the father is saying—we listen to what the father is saying. "I don't have the slightest idea, believe it or not. I think the name is probably out there somewhere in some specialized history book, but I never found out, you know."

Then you smile and stand up.

You still can't be certain that I am standing in front of the exit and that I'm opening today's copy of *El Mercurio* and reading the editorial page, but you smile anyhow and calmly go down the steps and say good-bye to the stewardess and walk firmly onward, carrying that bag with all your documents and that enormous blond doll, first through the passport line, where they stamp the page without a single question, just as always, then to claim your baggage—you point out the dark brown suitcase to the porter and he places it on top of the table in Customs, where it is inspected, the usual questions being asked while fingers explore beneath the clothes and in every nook and cranny with casual and passing interest, then the usual answers as well: you have nothing to declare, a few gifts, no liquor; you close the bag carefully and ably; the porter places your suitcase on his cart and to the question in his eyes you reply that you will take a taxi into the city, and you don't so much as glance at the two men who are standing by the exit, smoking. You will pay no attention to them, just pass by without even a nod in their direction. You're entering Chilean territory without a hitch, just as you did the first time, and every other time since then, and it is now, above my newspaper, that I see you at last, your body fills the horizon and blocks the light. After so much time only imagining you, it seems like a miracle that you really were on this flight, that it is you and not somebody else. I see you before you see me; you come out with the usual calm and composure, and before you catch sight of me, before you discover me sitting there in front of the exit, reading *El Mercurio* with the usual bored expression on my face, and I yawn beautifully and still don't deign to look at you, since I have both eyes stuck like pins into the two men who have still not moved from their position; even before you see me, your fear has gone and you're not even sure when it disappeared, and it's not going to return until the next trip, and maybe it has faded away forever, and now you are passing me, without so much as a hello or a see-you-later, first your suitcase goes by, then you with the bag, and it would have been beautiful to have been able to tell Arturo that I saw you at the same moment that you saw me, at that exact, precise, precious, mathematical, identical and illuminated instant, our eyes met without anyone else realizing it, but it's not true; I saw you first, the way it should be and now I keep on reading the paper, you're passing beside me, just inches from my body and now you know that there are no problems, and I also know that you were on the flight, as preestablished, and that you also have encountered no obstacles, because you have the bag hanging from your left hand and not the right, the bag that almost brushes against my knee as you pass; you know that everything has moved ahead smoothly in your absence, that this time you can again call the same Santiago phone number that they've given you in Buenos Aires and that you've memorized and that you would have had to forget with authentic primitive terror if Pedro, if I, were not there in the airport as usual to relieve your existence, if the two men had approached you cordially but with cold, hungry eyes. You know you can call that phone number that I of course do not know, so that they will pick you up on a corner which a voice will indicate to you, so that then they can take you to an apartment where you've never been before and where you'll never be again and where Arturo is undoubtedly awaiting you, and he will offer you a cup of coffee and one of his hand-rolled cigarettes and once the jokes have come to an end and a few questions about this and that, questions come and answers go, you'll hand him the doll, although he doesn't have a little girl either, and now you've already passed my side, right here where who knows how many years down the road I'll be once more, this time waiting for my son who will come back to his country when this whole nightmare is over, and now you've reached the taxi that's waiting for you, without even touching my arm from a distance; I can't even imagine what the warmth of your fingers would be like, or your voice when you're not talking to a porter, when you're not playing a role, you who only see me in this infinitely miserable little instant, I who watch you out of the corner of my eye and over a newspaper, every two months, you, a person with whom I've never exchanged so much as a syllable, not one devilish word, and whose real name I don't even want to guess at, just as you don't know anything about me, except that they call me Pedro and I read *El Mercurio* if everything's okay, and I have a big peaceful paunch and I wear glasses and that's all I need to do this duty, a newspaper and a yawn and a big peaceful paunch and one hell of an intuition to sniff out guys who stand at passenger exits smoking, and nerves of steel to let you know, wordlessly, that we're on schedule, that there are no delays, that the thing is moving ahead slowly but damned if it's not moving, that here I am in this airport seat, more solitary than ever, accompanied from a distance by you and by thousands like you whose names I don't know or even guess. I just tell you by my very presence that everything's fine, my lovely sister, welcome to Santiago again, we're okay, just great, I'll see you in another two months, until then, Monica; maybe some day I can really wait for you and jump up and hug you like the crazy man I am, earning that right for ourselves, too, until the next time, and now the taxi should be taking off and I don't turn my head, and you know, Monica, I was afraid, too, you know, even though I didn't tell Arturo when he hinted at it, I was afraid, too, *compañera*.

PUTAMADRE

"It's still not time," declared Putamadre. "They never open before eight."

The three of them reduced their stride and assumed a more measured rhythm that nonetheless retained the note of strength and pride that was there before, as if their legs had already guessed that they were on the right track, that that night they were going to have a great time, so what's the hurry, guys. As if to accentuate their bravado, their irreproachable freedom, their complete mastery of the pavements of that unknown city in a foreign land, the two largest of the young men had thrust their hands deep into their pants pockets and were entertaining themselves feeling the hidden, tense movement of those muscles strengthened by so many military calisthenics, muscles that were now climbing that hill with no apparent effort, muscles that, while they were not working very hard right now, later would be doing a real he-man's work and sweating like crazy. But the third one, who was slighter in build, couldn't keep still. He kept moving between the other two, trying to make a space for himself, unsure of where he should be. First he would work his way up to one side, then he'd edge up beside Putamadre, and finally he would elbow his way between them, stretching his neck so his head would reach the shoulders of the other two cadets in order not to lose a single rousing syllable of their conversation. He was just at the point of joining in with his own personal opinion, when Putamadre performed a bullfighter's turn, coming to a sudden halt and showing all his even, white teeth in a big grin. A blonde was passing by, swinging her hips as if some inner storm were stirring those soft thighs. He turned his head,

too, and made a valiant effort to come to an equally rapid stop.
Without success. He bumped into Putamadre, pushing him slightly.

"You clumsy kid!"

Putamadre brushed off his uniform with solemn dignity—there
wasn't to be a speck of dust on that immaculate deep navy blue.
He contemplated the blonde's magnificently flowing hips as she
disappeared down the street, his eyes expertly descending toward
the tanned legs and almost clinging, like a sail, to her skin.

"You would have to steer me off course, Valdés," Putamadre
pronounced. "Thanks to you, we've missed out on that blond mine-
sweeper."

Chico Valdés refused to discuss the violence of that judgment.
He was too interested in that woman. "Is she . . . ?"

Putamadre waited for the blonde to disappear completely into
the crowd before he answered. "She is," he sighed. "She and every
other broad. Right, Jorge?"

Jorge had not taken his hands out of his pockets even for an
instant. He appeared not to have the slightest interest in the
woman. He calmly agreed. "They're all whores, except for my
mother and my sister."

Putamadre let his mouth drop open like a drowning fish, then
stretched his lips so they were slightly twisted and squinted his
eyes into something that was more a sneer than a smile. "Oh, yeah,
of course, I forgot. Your mother and your little sister are different.
You'll have to forgive me." He swept off his cap with a flourish.
"Allow me to congratulate you, Your Majesty."

Chico saw his chance. "Every woman's somebody's mother or
somebody's sister," he said. He'd heard Putamadre himself say that
when they were gazing at the western coast of Colombia, waiting
for shore leave, about two weeks back. Two weeks. It didn't seem
possible. Two weeks. But now here they were, *the United States
of America*.

Jorge looked him up and down. "So what do you know about
these things? Huh? When did you get so in the know?"

"Let's move," urged Putamadre. "We're blocking traffic."

Jorge didn't budge. "Huh, Chico? So what do you know?"

"He doesn't know anything about it," said Putamadre. "That's
what we're here for, shithead. So he can learn."

"Okay," Jorge declared. "Okay. But this ass-brain should have himself a fuck first. Then he can talk like a man. Then he can stick his nose into somebody else's business."

"Let him think what he wants," said Putamadre. "It's a really big night in his life. Let him enjoy it." He made a sweeping gesture that took in the bay below, the Embarcadero and next to it the aristocratic silhouette of the tall ship, the large concrete buildings. "And what better place than San Francisco? It's almost like being back in Valparaiso. Like being at home. And these people are really great. Doing it for the first time here is almost like doing it in Chile. And besides it's more romantic . . ."

Chico was absorbed in examining a map of the city he had taken out of his pocket, trying to locate the corner where they were.

"What the hell you need a map for, smartass, when you've got me?" said Putamadre, snapping it out of his hand. "I know this place like the palm of my hand. We go to Fisherman's Wharf, but, instead of going along the waterfront like the other jerks, we go this way through downtown, see some of the sights, and you get a chance for a ride on the famous cable cars." He pointed to the street that continued on up the hill. "It's that way," he added. "Geary or Powell Street, I don't remember which of the two, but that's what I have a mouth for, to ask, well, to suck, too, but right now I'm going to ask the sixty-four-thousand-dollar question." He walked up to a tall young woman who was waiting at the corner for the light to change, and—winking an appreciative eye in the direction of his two friends—spoke to her in English. "Excuse me, miss, but we'd like to take the cable car to Fisherman's Wharf. In what direction?" The others were duly impressed with his pronunciation.

While she was answering him, Putamadre didn't take his eyes off her. Chico started to feel uncomfortable watching the way his friend stared deeply into those *gringo* eyes, blue, too pale and too transparent to stand that gaze. "Thank you," Putamadre said finally, parsimoniously. And then, "You're very nice." The girl flashed them a Colgate smile and crossed the street. Putamadre went on watching her. "It's just where I told you."

"Let's go then," said Jorge.

"Sure we're going," said Putamadre. "First stop, Fisherman's Wharf, real picturesque, like Puerto Montt but cleaner and more modern, and then we'll go down to Ghirardelli Square. There's lots of girls there and sometimes they take off their clothes right in the middle of the street. But there aren't as many hippies as there used to be." Putamadre led off in the direction of the street he had indicated. He took Chico Valdés by the arm. "I'm going to tell you a secret, Valdés. The best moment in every relationship is when you realize that the girl really wants it, she's ready, that all you have to do is push a little here and pull a little there, and you're home free. There's nothing like that moment, Chico. At that moment the course is clear; you know exactly what's going to happen. Everything else is anticlimactic. You get my drift?"

Putamadre had learned his first words in English with the rather British accent of Mackays Prep in Viña del Mar. Later he had perfected the language during the two years his parents had lived in Chicago. "Running away from that "*maricón* Allende" in his mother's terms. But a few months before the September Coup he had returned to Chile, flamboyantly enrolled in the Naval Academy. "How do you like my parents' foresight, huh? They knew for sure that Comrade Allende's days were numbered, that the man wasn't going to be there much longer. So I had to go back. A real shame. A pretty widow had fallen for me. I'd never made love to a woman that big before. A real giant of a *gringa*. All of a sudden there I am and I ask myself what I'm going to do with her. But they're all pretty much alike between their legs, whether they're elephants or dwarfs. The important thing is they like to screw, and if you know how . . ."

"How long were you in San Francisco?"

"Not long. I was here twice. Once on my way to L.A., and once on my way back. Long enough to memorize the opening and closing hours of the only place that matters."

"So if you're so cool, why don't we look for some really good girls, I mean girls that aren't whores," Jorge insisted. It wasn't the first time he'd said it. "In these uniforms it's a sure thing. All we have to do is show up and they'll fall all over us."

"In these uniforms it's a sure thing." Putamadre brought his hand with the fingers extended up to his chin as though he wanted to yawn, and then grimaced and gestured as if he were wiping the slobber from his mouth. "A sure thing. Show up and they fall all over us. Get off it! Don't you see we're with Valdés? Didn't we promise his uncle that he'd come back to Chile a real man? Have you forgotten they didn't let us off the ship in Colombia or in Ecuador, and we didn't even get into Acapulco because it was full of noisy, unpatriotic jerks, so we couldn't pick up anybody? You see it? We're horny, yeah, but we've got to go for a sure thing, because we've only got one night. Or do you want me to go off on my own and corner a pretty little dish, like that knockout we just saw, and leave you guys to fend for yourselves, huh?" They had reached the stop and Putamadre stood staring at them, his hands on his hips. "The one who's going to decide here is Chico Valdés. His opinion's the only one that counts."

"Well, I—" Chico said, but didn't finish, because at that moment the trolley stopped in front of them, its bells clanging.

"This is it," announced Putamadre. "All aboard, guys." He went on talking while they got on and he looked for the money to pay. "I'm going to take you to a real special place, a really far-out whorehouse. It's called Lucia's. Bilingual, no less."

"Bilingual?" asked Jorge. "Bilingual?"

"The madam who started it is an old whore descended from Mexicans. She named it after her mother, I think. What a surprise, right?" Putamadre handed over the money. "Three, please."

"In Spanish no less," said Jorge. "You're a real genius, Putamadre. Sometimes you're hard to take, but I have to give it to you, you're a genius."

"You're going to have a ball, Chico," Putamadre informed him. "Pan-American atmosphere. We'll pick out the best girl for you; we'll make them line up first and you choose the one you want and then show her what Chilean quality is all about."

"They could . . . Can they turn you down? Do they ever turn you down?" Chico Valdés could hardly form the question, although it finally came out, weakly, timidly, but it did come out, like a periscope in a stormy sea.

"They never turn you down," decided Jorge.

"All you need is the dough," added Putamadre, rubbing his fingers together meaningfully. "Everything can be bought in this life, old man, including love. That's what whores are for."

"The scum of the earth," said Jorge with a Belmondo-like air.

"What do you mean the scum of the earth? What do you mean? This is a real high-class place, good reputation, the girls are the cream of the cream, medical checks and greasing the police. Chico here can screw up a storm and not worry about getting the clap or anything like that." Putamadre put his arm across Chico's shoulders affectionately. "That's why they handed him over to me. And I keep my promises like a good sailor."

"Okay, fine," said Jorge. "Go ahead and defend your little cocksuckers, if you want to. You're in charge, Captain. This ship's on course for Lucia's. But I'll let you know later what I think about the merchandise."

"Give your opinion as much as you want," said Putamadre. "It's a free country. We're going back to the training ship *Esmeralda* with our balls empty, just in case we don't get another chance till we get to Tahiti, only native meat down there."

Jorge turned around in his seat. He studied Chico carefully. "Hey, Chico, what about you? Are you nervous?"

"What do you mean, nervous? He's a chip off the old block. With an uncle like his, he'll have no problem at all."

Chico didn't answer. Through the window a warm, gentle San Francisco twilight was visible. People were walking their dogs, shopping, on their way home, in no hurry, as if they considered themselves the lords of the universe. "The United States, old man." It was Putamadre's jubilant voice, and his hand patted Chico's shoulder with real emotion. Putamadre went on speechmaking. The center of the world, the most powerful country on earth. And more important, the country that had rescued their own, because when the rest of the cowards abandon ship, the Yankees always hang in there by their guns, with their missiles and their destroyers and their aircraft carriers, Putamadre in person assured them of that, and he knew them, he had lived with them for years right here on this generous soil, the *gringos* were the only allies you could count on, they hung in there with Chile, and with that kind of giant beside us nobody was alone in this world.

At that moment Chico pointed to a poster on a wall. What attracted his attention irresistibly was the name of Chile itself in big red letters, running like blood, like some deformed echo of what Putamadre had just said. He couldn't read the rest of it, but the colors were those of the Chilean flag, blue and white and more red. The trolley was moving too fast. They had already reached the top of the hill and were now on their way down, the immense San Francisco Bay sparkling below them.

"Look," he alerted them, but it wasn't necessary. Putamadre had suddenly swallowed all his praise. They could all make out several other posters, like a series of identical windows all along the street, culminating in a final sample, identical in design, that was just being put up on a new wall by a small group of *gringos,* two young guys and a blond girl, all of them moving somewhat nervously but efficiently. The trolley stopped a little farther on. They could see how the girl was gluing the edges of the poster with special care, almost affection. There could be no doubt about the message now. It wasn't exactly a welcome. They recognized their ship, the training vessel *Esmeralda,* sailing with its blue prow across a blood-stained sea, dead bodies in its holds and hanging from its masts, twisted figures, a screaming and distorted agony of men and women. The words were equally impressive. STOP THE TORTURE SHIP, they read. BOYCOTT CHILE.

"The motherfuckers," groaned Putamadre, savagely accentuating each syllable. "Right here in the U.S.A. The sons of bitches."

"They're everywhere," said Jorge. "Even here."

The trolley started to move away with surprising suddenness.

Putamadre took charge, "We're getting off," he ordered. "Now."

They rushed for the back door, but the conductor let them know dryly that they'd have to wait until the next stop. Something dangerous shone in Putamadre's eyes, but he controlled himself. They went the two blocks in silence.

Putamadre had scarcely touched the ground when he started resolutely back up the hill.

"What are you going to do?" Chico managed to ask.

But Putamadre's back remained imperturbable.

"Hey, Putamadre," said Jorge. "What do you plan to do?"

"We're going to beat the shit out of them," Putamadre announced, without slowing his pace. "We're going to show them that we won't just stand by and let them put up their dirty posters while there's a training ship of the Chilean Armada here."

"Just a minute, hold on a little," said Jorge. But it was as if Putamadre hadn't heard him. The other two had to make an effort not to break into a half-trot. "Listen, man, wait a minute, will you?"

Putamadre did not stop. He didn't even bother to look back. He shook off the arm with which Jorge was trying to slow him down.

"You tell him, Chico," said Jorge. "Tell him not to get into trouble, that he's in uniform."

"You're in uniform," said Chico. "We could get in a lot of trouble."

"The Commander told us not to let ourselves be provoked," added Jorge, now almost running beside Putamadre or just a little ahead of him, so that he could talk to him and gauge his reaction. "If we get into trouble, all the newspapers will pick it up and it'll be worse for us."

Putamadre came to a halt as brusquely as he had started up the hill, and turned to face them. "You goddamned cowards, yellow-bellied fag shitheads! Are you just going to stand by while a bunch of dirty, hairy-faced, Commie bastards soil the name of Chile? Chile may be small, but we have our pride. They're going to find out that our fight for freedom is still going on. I'm going to show them with these two arms, these two fists. After we've broken every bone in their bodies, then we'll rip all those posters to shreds. They're filling the whole damn city with . . . with . . ." He searched for words, but they failed him . . . "With shit," he said finally. "We don't have to put up with insults to our armed forces."

Jorge spoke slowly, trying to keep his voice steady. "If we so much as touch a hair on their heads," he said, "just imagine what'll happen if we so much as lay a hand on those guys."

"And what about the girl?" said Chico. "We can't fight with a girl."

"All I'm asking is that you think a minute, Putamadre. Calm down and think. The city's full of people who love and admire us and understand what happened in Chile, people who support us. We've got to think of them and not these jerks. They're the minority. We're in a friendly country, got it?"

Putamadre said nothing. His face wasn't as red as before, but his eyes were still full of the same ferocity that he had just poured out in that flood of words. He looked up the street, where the three people were putting up another poster. Just at that moment the rays of the setting sun were glistening on the cascade of golden hair that fell over the girl's shoulders and rippled down her back to her waist. She was dressed in a long skirt that reached her sandals. Her companions had long hair and beards and one on them was wearing a pair of those Trotsky glasses that a lot of hippies wear.

"Let's talk to them at least and explain things," Putamadre finally said. "We can't let them trick people with that pack of lies."

"We don't have time. Don't be an asshole," said Jorge. "They'll wake up on their own, when they don't have their daddy's money to live on and they have to work. That's what my mother always says and she's right."

Putamadre wouldn't give in. "Let's walk past them. So they'll see we're not afraid of them. Since I can speak English."

"That'll end up in a free-for-all," said Jorge. "And if something happens to us, we won't be able to keep our promise to Chico here. What's his uncle going to say then? I can tell you Captain Valdés is really going to be pissed."

All of a sudden Putamadre smiled, the way they do in the movies, with the bitterness of defeat, but at the same time the smugness of someone who's just understood some profound truth. He raised his head, took a deep breath, and looked at his two friends with infinite pity. "Okay, so we won't do anything to them. I promise. But . . ." and he squinted, almost closing his eyes completely, his thought was coming from so deep within him. "But . . . I want to find out where they live. Just in case we get the chance to pay them back sometime. Don't worry. I keep my promises. I'll wait here and then I'll follow them home. You guys take a little stroll. If you keep on down this street, you'll come to the Embarcadero and then we'll get together later in Ghirardelli Square."

Jorge and Chico could see that the young people were already moving away around the corner.

"We'll make a deal. If I don't manage to find out something within an hour and a half, then I'll give up. At quarter past eight, how's that? In Ghirardelli Square, the highest terrace." Putamadre was already moving off, beaming, calm, proud. He waved back at them. "I promise I'll behave myself. I won't screw that broad . . . this time at least." Without their being able to stop him, he ran toward the corner and turned in the direction the Americans had taken earlier.

"That asshole is crazy," Chico murmured.

"Crazy or not, he'll find out where they live. Their names, too. Just you wait."

———

They didn't have long to wait. He arrived at the place indicated at eight twenty-five. Jorge and Chico were sitting at a table on the terrace.

Putamadre greeted them from down the street with both arms raised.

"Having a ball, huh, guys? How'd it go? How did you make out without your favorite San Francisco guide, yours truly here?" And he pulled up a third chair.

"Did you get the information?"

"Did I get it? What are you guys having? Yeckkkkk! Forget the milkshakes. You should start off with the chocolate sundaes. They've got the best chocolate sundaes in the world here. That'll get us in shape for tonight. What we need is calories!"

Putamadre got up to order the sundaes personally.

"Look at that view, assholes," he said, suddenly possessed by an overwhelming and glorious surge of rage. "In Chile we'd be freezing our balls off right now and here we are watching the last rays of the sun on Frisco Bay. How do you like that?"

"You didn't do anything, right?" asked Jorge, worried at his friend's unexplained high.

"Eat your sundae and pay what you owe," Putamadre sang out. "I keep my promises, don't I? Have you ever known me to lie? Can a soldier break his code of honor? Huh? I didn't even touch that girl's little Commie tits. And I do mean they're little."

"What about the guys?" asked Chico.

"Them? Those sissy assholes? I wouldn't dirty my hands on queers like that. Those guys spend all day jerking off with their books. The only muscles they've got are in their eyelids." He stabbed at the sundae with his spoon and pulled out a big glob of ice cream. He rammed the whole thing in his mouth. "Hell, it's like we were in Valparaiso. But Valparaiso in the year 2000, when we'll have buildings and bridges like these. Look how blue that water is. Look at the Golden Gate. See, over there. That's what they call Sausalito. They have great parties."

"Come on. Tell us."

"There's nothing to tell. Her name is Marlene Jennings. She's single and lives alone. A student. Do you want to call on her? She lives at 126 Dolores Street, Apartment 2E. Everything here has a Spanish name."

"How'd you find out?"

Putamadre patted him gently on the cheek. "You pathetic kid. I followed them, you jerk. These *gringos* eat early. I know their customs. Missing a day like this, eating at home."

"What then?"

"And then? And then and then and then. I followed them, asshole. They went into that house. I asked about it in the store across the street."

Chico cleared his throat. "And they gave you the information, just like that?"

"Not just like that, Valdés. Nothing's free in this life. I latched on to the old lady who was working there and poured on a little Chilean charm."

"And she told you everything."

"Almost everything. The name was the really important thing. The *gringuita's* schedule. That's important, too. Do you want to know what time she comes home tonight, for example?"

Jorge followed the course of a sailboat that was crossing the bay. "What are their names?"

"Whose?"

"The guys."

"To hell with the names of those fairies. They probably couldn't fuck a sigh out of her. In that trio she's the big boss . . . And do you want to know how I know that? It's because she's a real cool chick, not one of these wide-assed, stupid *gringas* with buck teeth. Real tiny, but with a big voice, that's my little darling . . . I'd like to get you under the shower with all of your clothes off, you bitch. Too bad you're such a little agitator, such a little Communist cunt, but we can try to change your mind, can't we? Right? Once she gets a taste of what's really good, she won't treat her *Chilean boys* this way."

Jorge slurped the last drops of chocolate through a straw.

"Okay. You've had your good time. You know where she lives now. So let's mind our own business."

"Yeah," said Chico. "It's getting late."

"Here's the money. You go pay, Jorge," ordered Putamadre. "I'm not standing in line."

Jorge made no objection, even though there really was a long line in front of the cash register. As soon as Jorge had moved away, Putamadre leaned toward Chico.

"Okay, Valdés, how you feeling?"

"Fine. Why should I feel bad?"

Putamadre bit his lip and looked pensive. "After the first time, you change, you know. You're never the same anymore."

"I'm not afraid."

"We cadets are never afraid," said Putamadre. "Your mom just didn't know how to raise you, that's the problem." It was getting dark. Some lights were coming on around the square. "I want to ask you something, Chico. Now, before, I mean, you know?"

Chico said nothing.

"Look, I'm your friend, Chico. I'm an ensign, but you can trust me. You know I don't like to stick my nose in other people's business. If you don't like what I'm going to say to you, you just say so, just like that, like a real man, and that'll be the end of it. But there's just one question I'd like to ask you, just so I can really help you tonight, so everything will go smoothly."

"We've already talked a lot," said Chico. "All during the trip, all day long, all we talked about was girls."

"You didn't get me."

"I'm tired of listening to stories. How many days is it since we left Valparaiso, forty or something like that, and every day you've told me a different story."

"I thought it'd do you good to listen to an expert, you'd find out all the details, you'd see how natural the whole thing is, and you wouldn't be so shy."

"Okay. So I'm not so shy anymore. I know exactly how you laid that farmer girl, the first one, on your grandfather's estate, and how it's always a good idea to have a handkerchief with you, in case she's a virgin. And all about that Nelly character, the store clerk with the two-ton tits and—"

"Stuff it a minute. I don't want to tell you any more stories. You didn't get me. I just want to ask you one little question."

Chico stood up. Jorge was coming back, so they moved toward the stairs.

"What's the matter with Chico?" asked Jorge. "Did you say something to him?"

Putamadre took him by the arm. "You blew it, you son of a bitch. You came back too soon. Leave this to me . . . Look, you just follow us, back aways, like something else catches your attention. A few magic moments and . . . presto! We'll have Valdés all ready for the big event."

Jorge was dropping the change, coin by coin, into Putamadre's open hand, his eyes fixed on his friend's face. He let them fall slowly, on purpose.

"You're such a big mouth, Putamadre. What'd you tell the poor guy?"

Putamadre's expression did not change. He dropped the change into his pocket, producing a jingling sound. "Look, Jorge, I've helped break in half the school, so don't try to teach me how to do this. I just have to find out something, that's all."

"What?"

Putamadre gestured toward Chico, who was leaning on the balustrade, looking at the lush sunset over the bay. A light breeze relieved the heat, at the same time swelling the sails scattered across the water.

"There's something he never told us about that little problem he had."

"Oh. You're still stuck on what happened."

"Yeah. What happened. That girl, what was she like, physically, I mean? What was she like?"

"You never give up, Putamadre. We don't know what she's like. I hoped Captain Valdés would finally manage to identify her."

"Captain Valdés insists that Chico refuses to even mention the whole thing. Naturally, Chico's embarrassed, I mean, since he couldn't get it up that night . . ."

Jorge lit a cigarette. "And Chico's never told you anything?"

Putamadre breathed deeply, filling his lungs with the soft sea air, air that was gradually cooling off, announcing the approach of nightfall, but where there still remained a taste of sunlight. "Of course he's told me. He's told me everything."

"Everything?"

"Almost everything. What we already know: that he didn't want to push her, that it wasn't fair, or something like that, that she was defenseless, and that it just wasn't right. That she had a right to her own ideas. Bullshit! He was with the chick a long time, talking, I guess. What an asshole. Somebody else probably laid her later."

"But he's never described her to you."

"Chico's real close-mouthed. Tight as a clam. Besides, that night was a real mess, you remember. I don't remember myself whether I laid the same girl twice or if they were two different broads. How were we to guess that Chico would freeze up when it was his turn? Could I guess that?" Putamadre looked at Chico, who was still absorbed in viewing the intermittent blue motion of the sea captured there in the gulf, the first lights of the cities breaking the peaceful vista, and the coffee-brown and green hills that spread out beyond. The shadow of San Francisco's skyline spread over the water like a gentle gust of darkness. "But he's going to tell me; he's going to tell me everything. You can't keep secrets from Putamadre. He finds out everything in the end."

"If I were you, I'd leave Chico alone. He's pretty jumpy. Don't pressure him too much."

"The point is, I'm not you. Maybe you haven't realized that yet. I'm me. I'll be gentle with him." He winked a big eye at Jorge and walked toward Chico, elbowing his way into place beside him. For a while he said nothing, sharing the view, the boats, the noise of passersby, the skirts of females who were strolling below them to the eternal joy of eyes like theirs. "You don't have to get so pissed off, Chico."

"I'm not pissed off."

"You're pissed off, all right, and you have a right to be. Look, Chico, I know myself, hell, I know myself like there was a mirror in front of me all the time. I know I'm always running off at the mouth; I never give anybody a chance to get a word in edgewise."

Chico tried to concentrate on a seagull and did manage to follow its endless and sleepy flight. When it disappeared, he said, "Everybody has his own personality. You're not responsible for the luck of the draw."

"That's the reason I don't want to be talking all the time, understand. I'd rather listen to you. But it's hard for me to listen."

"The thing is, Putamadre, you have a hell of a lot to tell; that's why you talk so much. Me, on the other hand, I've never really lived. Especially since my old man died, it's like life came to a standstill. Just me and my mom in that house."

"Okay. But entering the Naval School was a great idea. That was a good move on your uncle's part."

"My uncle always wanted me to be a navy officer like him. It was my dad who thought there was no future in it."

"With all due respect, there's nothing better, Valdés. It's the best thing there is. Nothing but future." Putamadre looked all around, as if searching for an audience for his next words. He put his hand on the back of his neck and stretched toward the sky, enjoying the cracking of his muscles, the tension in his chest, his elbows pushing forcefully against the air.

"It's all the same to me," said Chico. "It's a career like any other."

"Like any other? It's the queen of all careers. No, what am I saying? That's a lie. It's the empress. And now more than ever, having to take care of the country."

"The country," Chico repeated.

"Yeah, the country, man. What you can't seem to get into your thick skull, Chico, is that we're heroes, national heroes . . . With your brain, Chico, and your sensitivity, you could end up as Minister of Education some day. That ministry belongs to the Navy, right?"

"And you're going into Relations abroad, right?" asked Chico, with a hint of mockery in his voice.

"I go for all kinds of relations, man, abroad, two broads, whatever turns up."

They laughed and a certain tired electricity between them diminished as though someone had thrown a circuit breaker. They started walking, in no great hurry, going down the first steps. Behind them, Jorge appeared to be totally absorbed in watching a little boy who was bouncing a ball and catching it.

"You know what, Putamadre, I'm not a bit nervous," said Chico.

"Of course not," answered Putamadre.

"The problem is I just don't believe much in words. You don't get anywhere just talking and talking and talking. You get fed up, you know? First we were going ashore in Colombia, then it was Ecuador. And Acapulco. Acapulco wasn't an official call. Acapulco was a sure thing. I got prepared every time, just the way you told me to; I thought about her, went over every inch of her body in my mind, from head to foot."

"Slowly. You gotta do it slowly," urged Putamadre. "But making sure not to think about that one most important thing."

"Right. Making sure not to think of that one most important

thing. I just let myself go, getting psyched, relaxing, deep-breathing, so everything would go fine. Sometimes I had trouble going to sleep at night, Putamadre. That tropical heat. But we never went ashore. Nothing but official receptions. And you know something? I really liked one of the girls, the young women, at one of those dances in Colombia."

"But they're not for screwing," objected Putamadre. "They're real classy. People like us."

"I was crazy about one of them," Chico insisted. They were still descending the steps that led to the street. They were endless. Their footsteps resounded in military unison. Their black shoes, polished to perfection, sparkled as if they were on parade. "We never got ashore," repeated Chico. "We were stuck there, staring at the land, the houses, the damn pier. All leaves canceled, boys. It's dangerous, boys. There's a demonstration against Chile, boys. National security, boys. And there you were with your damned stories." He looked at his friend out of the corner of his eye and quickly added, "I appreciate it, Putamadre, I really do, but just imagine how I feel, how I felt. The shit was piling up inside me and had no way to get out. Even when we were doing exercises and you were training us, telling us to shake our asses, to shake our asses as if we had our favorite lover under us. I felt like hell."

"It's true," Putamadre agreed. "You're absolutely right. I'm always running off at the mouth. But that's the way I was born, what do you want me to do?"

Chico pushed up his sleeve and showed him his watch, accusingly. "You said at eight o'clock and it's nine now. We'd be there by now if you hadn't gotten the bright idea of following some stupid *gringa*."

"Not a stupid *gringa*. She was pretty. You saw her." Since Chico didn't answer, Putamadre took advantage of the opportunity. "That's just what I wanted to talk to you about, I mean I wanted to ask you that question, and then we'll go and hoist up the school's flag. And I mean hoist the thing up."

Chico didn't laugh this time. They had reached the street, and he stopped walking, as if they both agreed that this was the corner to hold a conversation. "What's basic is to know how to choose the right girl tonight," Putamadre went on. "And I need more information."

"She just has to be a woman, that's all," said Chico. "Let's stop kicking this around."

"You have to feel right with the broad, Valdés. I'm telling it like it is. I know what I'm talking about. I need to know more about what that girl was like, the one that night. That's what I have to ask you about."

Chico took a deep breath. "I've already told you I just didn't feel like making love to a woman who didn't want to. I know that seems old-fashioned."

"But I'm not saying anything about that. Everybody to his own taste. That's why we live in a free country. As far as I'm concerned those sluts deserve whatever they get. I don't need to lay bitches who were for Allende. I've got lots of other beds waiting for me."

"That may be, but you screwed them that night just like everybody else."

"They were giving it away, man, fresh meat and for free. What I'm saying is I didn't really need it. It was a good opportunity and I grabbed it. Those things always happen in wartime. It's the victor's booty. If they'd won, every lousy one of them would have been grabbing our women, and I don't mean in the Naval School. I mean in our own homes."

"I couldn't. That's all," said Chico.

"So who's saying anything, man. I just think you blew a golden opportunity. And you sure didn't do that girl any favor, because somebody else grabbed her. And I can tell you he didn't waste time on scruples . . . And those girls had a great time that night; they saved their skins and we let them go later. I know what I'm telling you."

"They were saved?" asked Chico.

"They're all whores," said Putamadre. "The one I had ended up enjoying it like hell."

Chico put his hands in his pockets and kicked a pebble that hit a lamppost. It made a metallic sound and bounced off. "Putamadre, I don't believe you. I just don't believe that."

"Believe me if you want and if you don't, then go screw yourself. I'm telling you, it's a matter of biology. If you just tingle her little button, if you know where she likes to be rubbed, if you move your ass the right way, if you wait till the right moment, then our sweet Eve will explode, she'll explode, man, that's all there is to it. These bitches are all whores. They like it, man, they like it."

"Putamadre," said Chico, "could I ask you a big favor?"

"All you've got to do is ask, Valdés. Your wish is my command."

"Putamadre, let's get going."

"Okay. Let's go. It's not far. Near Nob Hill." Putamadre tried one last attack. "But it would really help me if you'd describe that girl . . . It's the best way to really get the most out of this experience, understand? At least her hair, Valdés, just tell me that, so I can tell your uncle I knew how to make the right choice."

"Why don't you let him choose?" said Jorge, who at that moment had caught up with them.

Putamadre turned on him furiously. "You stay out of it."

"I'm in it and so what?" said Jorge. "Valdés is a friend of mine, too. I can give him advice just like you."

They were of about the same build, but Putamadre appeared to be about three feet taller at that moment. He spoke from above him, like an admiral giving orders. "Captain Valdés talked to me. He entrusted me with this mission. I'm responsible; I gave my word of honor as a cadet and I intend to carry it out. And what's more, I'm going to carry it out to perfection. So you stay out of it, and as for you, Chico, you're going to tell me what color hair that girl had."

"None of this is important," said Chico.

"Look, Valdés," said Putamadre. "Valdés, I want to know if she was a blonde. It may seem an insignificant detail to you, but I want to know. Tell me and then we'll go."

"Leave him alone."

"You shut up. This is between Chico, his uncle and me. If we decided to invite you for the party, be happy about that and keep quiet . . . Valdés!"

"This is a bunch of crap," said Chico. "There's nothing to describe."

"Was she a blonde? Or brunette? At least tell me that."

Chico hesitated for a moment. It was dark and a swarm of small black flies were buzzing around the neon lights.

"She was a blonde," Chico said finally.

"She was a blonde." Putamadre flashed a broad smile, and rubbed his hand across his well-groomed hair. "Okay, Valdés. That's great, because it'll make our mission a lot easier. Let's move out, assholes.

What the hell are we doing standing here?" They started walking. "Was she a natural blonde?"

"Natural," said Chico. "A university student. At least she had been. They had just expelled her. It seems one of her parents had been an immigrant."

"It looks to me like you know a lot about her," said Putamadre. "If you had laid her . . . But forget that. It's a new ballgame. All brave men, follow me."

They walked in silence for several minutes. Putamadre was whistling, humming and feinting at lampposts, all the while singing the praises of San Francisco. He was drunk with happiness, running over with a power that surged through him like electricity. The other two followed him without a word.

"It's this way. Didn't I tell you?" proclaimed Putamadre, jubilant. He had just checked it out with a band of kids who were sadly watching an improvised game of basketball on a nearby court. "Your old man here has a memory like a . . ."

The building was tall, modern and imposing. Beyond the impeccably clean glass doors an elegant vestibule was visible: a discrete row of houseplants and vines stood before a long mirror and added to the sense of a select and distinguished ambience. The only thing missing was the doorman.

"Third floor, B," announced Putamadre, and pressed the button.

"Is it here?" asked Jorge, amazed.

"It's a high-class joint. I wouldn't bring you to some low-class whorehouse."

Just then they heard a woman's voice from the intercom, speaking English: "What's the name?"

Putamadre answered in English that he'd been there before, about two years ago, and that there were three in the party.

"Okay," said the voice, and they heard the prolonged sound of the buzzer.

"You stay here," said Putamadre, pushing the door open. "I'll be back in a flash."

"I'm going with you," said Chico.

"We go up together," pressed Jorge, "or none of us goes up."

Putamadre did not answer. The elevator was roomy, silent, and fast. The door to apartment 3B was half-opened. Putamadre knocked softly and they went in.

There was no one waiting for them in the entry hall, which was scarcely lighted. In the semi-darkness they could make out two doors, both closed. From the other side of one of them they could hear the sound of glasses, a sustained whisper of voices, and above the conversation a woman's sharp and strident laughter. They heard, as though from a great distance, the first measures of a song. In Spanish. *"Cuando te veo con la blusa azul . . ."* It was a bouncy song, but there was also a note of defeat in it, a sadness that swept over them suddenly. *"Mis ojos sin querer van hacia ti . . ."* Putamadre, beaming, claimed the hall with a broad gesture of his hands. But his voice came out fragile and low, as if they were in a cemetery or a hospital.

"So what do you say? There's the bar and the room where we can dance a little and look over the merchandise. You have to invite the girls to a few drinks. That's why we've got these fat bills, the good Yankee dollar. Later we go over there," and he pointed toward the second door, "where we can test the quality of the mattresses."

"What are we waiting for?" asked Jorge. "Let's go in."

"Just a moment. A little patience please, my little lions. We have to wait here. I'm sure Lucía will receive us in person. She always comes out to take a look first."

At precisely that second, the door that led to the bar opened. The brunette who entered the hall was tall, very tall and slender, dressed in rather somber colors, but in the latest style, to be sure, and of uncertain age, as if she had decided, upon reaching maturity, to freeze that moment forever and not to grow any older, but also as though certain parts of her body had not obeyed her completely. "Come in, come in," she said. "Make yourselves at home."

"We speak Spanish," said Putamadre. *"Hablamos español."*

"Welcome in Spanish, then," the woman said, in Spanish, with a heavy Mexican accent.

"Isn't Lucía here?" asked Putamadre.

All of a sudden the woman looked at them differently; they felt themselves being scrutinized by her intense eyes in that darkness. It was as if she had suddenly remembered something. "No, Lucía isn't here," she said. "She's in Bakersfield." But her words came from someplace far away, emptied of content, as though she were thinking of something else. She still had her fingers on the doorknob, but she didn't open the door to let them in. To the contrary, she closed it. The already insufficient light grew dimmer and the fragmentary impression of smoke, music, a special density that circulated there inside, where they had been able to glimpse men and women dancing, drinking, laughing, disappeared. The only thing they could still hear clearly was the imperious, imploring voice of the singer: *"Por Dios no te pongas más, la blusa azul."* And then the chorus of voices: *"Por Dios no te pongas más, la blusa azul."* "Did you come into the port today?" asked the woman.

"We got here yesterday," answered Jorge. "But we just now got off the ship."

"Of course," said the woman, "and you came straight here."

Something strange was going on, something indefinable and cold was taking shape in the corners and along the walls of this room. The woman went up to the switch and turned on the light. The brutal, deadly light caused them to blink, and they suddenly saw themselves in a mirror that dominated the space between the two doors. There they were, in their immaculate uniforms, perfect, overwhelming specimens of masculinity. Splendid, impeccable, irreproachable. Putamadre was the first to break the silence. He saw himself speaking in the mirror and admired his own serenity.

"Not directly here, no," he said. "We took a little walk first. You don't open until eight, so what was the point to hurry."

"You were here before," said the woman. "I don't remember you."

"I was here twice," said Putamadre. "Both times with Tomasa. I don't remember you either."

The woman remained calm. She had an unlit cigarette in her left hand, but made no move to light it. She didn't come any closer to them and she didn't open the door. The distance that separated them was shocking and frozen, as if a dead cat were obscenely sprawled there between them and the woman and nobody wanted to take the first step over it.

"Is Tomasa here tonight?" asked Putamadre.

"Tomasa went back to Mexico."

"So there'll be others," said Putamadre. "A shame. I liked her a lot . . . Well, let's go in." But he didn't move, once again waiting for her to invite them.

"You're from Chile." It wasn't a question, but rather an affirmation.

"Yeah. From Chile," declared Putamadre. "And proud of it. Three Chileans with well-padded wallets and ready for a good time." He looked at the others. "Right?"

"We've been on ship a long time," said Jorge.

"And what about that uniform? Do you always wear it? Or do you leave it home sometimes?"

"We're cadets," explained Jorge. "Don't think that we're part of any crew."

"Right," said the woman. "You can see that you're real gentlemen and know how to treat women. You came on that sailing ship with the pretty name. I had a friend in Mexico by that name. Esmeralda."

But she didn't move, didn't make the least motion to open the door for them, to smile at them, or anything. It was as if the four of them were waiting for a bus and were chatting to pass the time.

Putamadre decided to take the bull by the horns. After all, he was responsible for this expedition. "What's going on? Aren't there any girls? Are they all busy?"

"It's not that," she said.

"Because if you're busy, we'll come back later. We're in no hurry."

"It would be easy to tell you that's the reason," she said with her slightly hoarse Mexican voice. "But that's not it."

"Great," said Putamadre. "Then we all agree."

At that moment the side door opened and a couple appeared and crossed the hall, laughing, toward the salon. Hanging on the arm of a fiftyish and balding *gringo* was a really fantastic blonde, wild, phenomenal, contained in a green dress that looked like a second skin. She was a white panther, wrapped in a dizzying aroma of perfume, radiating torrid waves of energy in every direction, from her lips, her breasts, her hips, a real momument to nature. The three of them stood there staring at her until she disappeared.

"No deal," said the woman. "Too bad, boys."

"What?" said Putamadre. "What's too bad?"

The blonde stuck her head through the door. "Hey, what's the matter? Everybody's asking for you, Sylvia. You're the life of the party."

"It's the guys from Chile," said the woman.

"Oh," said the blonde. "The Chileans. The sailor boys." She glided into the hall with incredibly feline movements. She gazed at them with her enormous eyes, one by one, and it was as if someone were bathing them in champagne, as if they were bubbling warmly in somebody's throat.

"She doesn't speak Spanish, but she understands," said the woman. "She can explain everything." And then to the blonde, in English: "You want to tell them?"

"It's a strike, boys," said the blonde. "Sorry." She approached Jorge, took his hand and examined it as if it were a rare object. She brushed her finger along his life line, and then made the sign of the cross in his palm.

"Say it in Spanish," said the woman. "Speak to them in their language."

With her other arm the blonde hung from Putamadre's neck. She rocked like that for a while, both hands occupied, like a bridge between the two cadets. "Come here, you, lonely boy," she said to Valdés, who wasn't being held anywhere. Chico didn't budge.

Putamadre took her by the waist. "And you, love, what's your name?"

"*Huelga*," said the blonde in Spanish. The word slipped out with a *gringo* accent, but as clear as a bell or like a wheatfield in the sun, as if she had been slaving for hours over a dictionary, studying its pronunciation.

"*Huelga?*" Jorge repeated, as if he didn't understand that language.

"*Huelga*," the blonde insisted. "We're on *huelga*. Don't you know what that means?" She sketched the "h" for him on the front of his uniform and then the rest of the letters. "*Huelga*—that means strike."

"But how come?" protested Putamadre. "What about those guys inside, why are you tending to them?" He pulled his arm from around her waist furiously. "I've never heard of anything like this in my whole life . . . it's . . . ridiculous."

"It's not a strike against everybody," said the woman called Sylvia, eventually. "It's just against you."

"Against us? Against sailors?"

"No. Against you, the Chileans on the *Esmeralda*. That's all."

"Nothing tonight for any of you boys, not here in Frisco," said the blonde, twisting the lock of hair that fell across Putamadre's forehead around her finger. *"Nada, nada."*

Putamadre pulled his head away and stepped back to get out of the woman's reach. "Against us? Just against us?"

"If you want to come back another day, when the ship's gone, we'll be happy to have you here again. As long as you aren't wearing uniforms, our house is yours whenever you're in San Francisco. But not tonight."

Chico Valdés spoke up for the first time. "When the ship leaves," he said slowly, "we go with it. We can't stay here when it lifts anchor."

"That's the thing, that's what I'm trying to explain." The woman contemplated them with her impassive eyes, eyes that had seen everything, that had done everything. "The exit's that way, boys." Since no one moved, she went through the door herself and walked toward the elevator. She pressed the button. "We're on strike. The assembly made the decision two days ago. Boycott the *Esmeralda.* We always carry out our democratic decisions."

"Democratic," Putamadre exploded. "Whores, democratic? The whole world's gone crazy!"

Inside, the record was coming to an end. The blonde was singing along in a low voice, with an impossibly bad accent. *"Por Dios no te pongas más la blusa azul. Por Dios no te pongas más, la blusa azul."*

"Are we going to leave?" asked Jorge. "Are we going to let them throw us out like this?"

The elevator had arrived. The woman called Sylvia opened the door for them and for the first time she smiled at them, almost maternally, more like a Madonna smiling at her baby than anything else. With her dark hair and those black eyes in that bronze face, she almost seemed Chilean. "That's life, kids," she said. "You learn something new every day."

Putamadre walked toward the entrance to the apartment. He was clenching and unclenching his fist in rage and his lips were trembling. But when he spoke, his voice came out calm, manly, and in a cowboy baritone. "This doesn't strike me as the best way to hold on to your customers," he said.

The blonde released Jorge's hand. "Bye-bye, boys."

"It doesn't strike me as a very good way to hold on to your

customers," Putamadre repeated, looking first at the blonde and then at Sylvia.

"There are more important things," said Sylvia, and pointed toward the elevator. "Why don't you go on home, boys. We're wasting our time. Not tonight."

Putamadre turned his back on her. He looked at his two friends and raised his voice. "Now you see what happens when governments go soft. Even the whores rebel on us and turn into Communists." He motioned with his head, as if he were commanding a combat squadron. "Let's go look for someplace else. Frisco is full of houses."

Sylvia's voice reached him, tired and scarred, but determined. "You won't find anyplace that'll accept you. There's not a girl in San Francisco. Not even if you offer her a fortune. Not even the oldest, the ones hanging out in the alleys. Nobody will stoop that low."

Putamadre took his time. He walked up to the blonde and said to her, "One of these days I'll come back here and show you a thing or two, girlie. If you're still here." Then he moved slowly toward the elevator. Chivalrously, he allowed his friends to enter first. Then he entered, and Sylvia closed the door. For a fleeting moment the ripe bronze glow of her face was captured in the small round window of the elevator, like the portrait of some forgotten Aztec goddess. "Be seeing you," promised Putamadre. Then, composed, he pushed the button and she disappeared from view. They went down in silence.

"The scum of the earth," said Jorge, suddenly, and kicked the elevator door open. "The scum of the earth."

Putamadre remained silent. He smiled with a docility that was rare in him.

"We should have told them something," Jorge went on. "We should have given them hell, Putamadre. We should have said something."

"Could what she said be true?" Chico wondered. "Could it be true that in the whole city of . . ."

They walked out into the street. Putamadre glanced back toward the third floor, but they could hear nothing, not even music. He lit a cigarette, striking the match against the wall. "What time is it, Chico?" he demanded.

"Let those goddamned bitches shit all over us!" said Jorge. "Shit in our faces."

"Damn it, kid, what time is it?" Putamadre ordered once more.

Chico held his watch so they could see it. It was almost ten. Putamadre stopped under a streetlight. He kept his eyes on the third floor, through the drifting smoke as it rose toward the balcony of 3B.

"Letting them insult us like that," said Jorge. "Scum, garbage, the pits. A goddamned bitch treating us like that! A whore!"

Putamadre shook his head pensively. His calm was extraordinary. "So she was a blonde, huh?"

Chico made no answer.

"Like our little *gringa,* kid? Just tell me that. Was she like our *gringa?*"

"*Gringa?*" asked Jorge. "What *gringa?*"

Chico paid no attention to Jorge. He was staring fixedly at Putamadre. His voice was shaking. "Yeah, a lot like her. The same long hair."

"Was she more or less the same build, Chico? Slender, with nice hips, lots to hang on to, small tits?"

Chico didn't answer.

"Who are you guys talking about?" Jorge interrupted them again. "Who the hell are you talking about?"

"You don't have to answer my question, Chico," Putamadre went on. "I know she was about the same. Right?"

Quietly, Chico replied, "Yeah. Just about."

"Would you mind telling me who you're talking about?" asked Jorge.

Putamadre ignored him. "It's not so late," he said. "And it's not far." He placed both hands on Chico's shoulders and breathed deeply. "What do you think, Chico?"

"I don't think," said Chico. "I don't think at all."

"If you're worrying about the uniform," said Putamadre, "in this darkness nobody will know."

"I don't think," Chico repeated. "And it's not because of the uniform. It has nothing to do with the uniform."

"Look, Valdés," said Putamadre. "I made a promise to your uncle, Valdés."

Jorge intervened again. "Would you mind telling me what you're talking about? I don't understand a damned thing!"

Chico shook his head.

"We don't even have to turn on the light," said Putamadre. "We won't even say a word . . . Chico! They've got to pay up once and for all, the bastards."

Chico kept on shaking his head, as if he no longer trusted his voice to come out—like a stubborn horse who has forgotten any other movement.

"Your old man here will arrange everything. Barrenechea and me will fix everything for you. Right, Jorge?"

"Fix what?" said Jorge.

"In case you still haven't caught on," said Putamadre as if he were talking to an idiot, "the topic of conversation is the *gringa*."

"What *gringa*?" Then Jorge said: "Oh. That *gringa*."

"You win a prize," said Putamadre. "That *gringa*. That's what it's all about. We gave our word that he'd be a man when he got back to Chile, and we're going to deliver."

"You're the one who gave his word," said Jorge. "I didn't promise anything."

Putamadre threw the cigarette onto the pavement. "Chico, these *gringos* leave their windows open in the summer. We'll wait for her in her apartment, Chico. She'll be coming in alone tonight, about eleven o'clock. It'll be easy. And nobody can connect us with her. Easy. Right, Jorge?"

"It's not easy," said Jorge, and his voice was trembling. "But it's not impossible either."

"How long are we going to put up with it, Chico? Huh? An eye for an eye. An ass for an ass. That's my philosophy."

Chico went on shaking his head, staring at the ground and avoiding Putamadre's eyes. His gaze was fixed on the cigarette that was burning at his feet.

"Barrenechea," said Putamadre. "You talk to him, Barrenechea. Explain it to him."

Jorge smiled slightly. "Come on, kid," he said. "The day comes to all of us when we have to be a man. You'll feel better. Putamadre is right. It'll be easy."

Putamadre mashed the cigarette butt with his foot. Then he

squeezed Chico's shoulders until the boy had no choice but to meet his eyes.

"What do you think, Chico? Are we going? Huh? Are we going to have some fun at the *gringa*'s place? With our sweet little blond Marlene?"

They waited for an answer.

LONELY HEARTS COLUMN

Dear Tormented Patriot:

In spite of the obvious interest it holds for our readers, we are unable to publish your letter due to its excessive length. In any case, you are not as abandoned and alone as you seem to believe. Keep on having faith and don't be surprised if the solution to your dilemma is just around the corner. I will write to you personally to offer you some valuable advice.

Affectionately,
Rosalyn

(From an edition of the newspaper *Las últimas noticias,*
April 18, 1974, page 22, column 24.)

April 14, 1974

Dear Rosalyn:

Not even in the worst moments of my life did I ever think I would be writing to you. If I am now turning to you for your highly esteemed advice, it is because I find myself in a dead-end street and have no one to turn to. I'm sure that you will be able to help me, as, year after year, you have been helping so many other trouble-ridden representatives of the weaker sex.

As a woman, as a Chilean and as the mother of three children, I fought the government of Señor Allende with determination, expecting no other prize than to be governed by men of decency and of irreproachable morality. Everyone in my neighborhood can vouch for the way I organized the women in the struggle against the ration cards, a maneuver by which the Communists wanted to subjugate our souls through our stomachs. Fortunately the clamor of all the free voices of this nation did not go unheard. Chile had its conscience, and the righteous instrument of that conscience, our glorious armed forces, carried out our most intimate will, rising up as one man. I repeat that we never dreamed of any other benefit than the one which, in effect, came to us: the return to normalcy, to the peace of our homes and the laughter of our children, playing happily in their yards with no fear of degenerates and snipers.

Nevertheless, I did receive an additional and unexpected reward after the military takeover. The ways of God are mysterious, but certain, and all my sufferings, my efforts on behalf of the Fatherland, brought me a personal prize. Not only was the national reconciliation, which I so desired, brought about, but also something was settled in the bosom of my own family. To make a long story short, the Lord returned my husband to me, using the military junta as intermediary.

Ever since the institution of the curfew, he has been restored to me. Before, our life together was hell. He would come home at all hours of the night, and, although he is not one of those men who drink excessively, I was sure that he was seeing other women. I never caught him, to tell the truth, but he was always euphoric when he came home so late. The few hours he spent with me were terrible. He always wanted to be somewhere else, no doubt to see his "girlfriends." When I remonstrated with him about his attitude, never mentioning "them," of course, he always responded with political attacks, insulting me with accusations of being "reactionary" and "ignorant" and other such epithets. It reached the point where he asked me, in fact begged me, for a separation once and for all, a thing which I could not accept then and would never accept now. And not just because of the demands of my religious upbringing as a good Catholic, but also because I have real affection for him. We haven't spent twelve years together, in good times and in bad, for nothing. The problem was that the man had become too politicized. His women egged him on, stirred up his enthusiasm to become even more involved in the "revolution." Before Allende, it wasn't like that. What had happened to his love?

Our arguments got more and more bitter. He didn't like my being so active in the neighborhood. Don't interfere in what you don't understand, he told me. I was trying to find out the names of the militias they were arming. They were up to something. Later I found out it was the famous ZETA plan, in which they were going to cut all our throats; I was on the list, too, according to what the lady in the local store told me.

What are my *compañeros* going to think, he would ask me, and he was furious when I announced that I was going to participate in the march of the empty pots and pans. *Compañeros!* They were a bunch of good-for-nothings and cowards, I told him. They had stolen him from me. It was easy for the men to support Señor Allende. They didn't have to stand in line for ten hours to get a bottle of oil or two pounds of sugar. So I kept up my patriotic duties all during 1972. Once he even threatened me physically and if it were not for the intervention of our neighbor, a widower who is a truck driver, I don't know what would have happened. You might know he would be a truck driver, my husband said the next day, when he had calmed down. Yes, I answered him proudly, one of the truck drivers, ready to help me just as they came to the aid of the country last October, paralyzing this land with their strike.

But my husband refused to listen to reason. I decided to keep quiet just to preserve what little peace there was in our home. All through the summer of 1973 he continued to come home very late; he had been painting walls, he would say. As if he could have been painting until four in the morning! But what good did it do for me to throw up to him the fact that nobody respected the law, that you couldn't go downtown anymore because the only thing you could breathe was tear gas, that even chickens were scarce now, when the ones responsible for everything were the very criminals that he admired so much, occupying the highest public posts? What good did it do to evoke tearfully the image of our two daughters at the mercy of hordes of barbarians, to tell him they would take our house away, that people in the neighborhood were saying that the President himself engaged in practices that were contrary to decorum and decency? They had poisoned his mind; no argument produced any effect.

My only satisfaction was in clearly making my cross on the ballot in the March '73 elections next to the name of Colonel Labbé, to see if things would finally be straightened out. I always had faith in the military.

But things just got worse. In spite of my discretion, he became more and more distant, until by the middle of 1973, around July, he told me he was looking for a small apartment to move into. If you could have heard the hatred in his voice. The words still hurt me. He said he couldn't stand living with me anymore, that he was ashamed of me. I made no attempt to dissuade him. I wrapped myself in my own dignity, because, after all, I was not about to grovel. So, if he wanted to leave, what could a poor, defenseless woman do, especially when he had accomplices in the government of the Republic?

Everything changed on September 11, 1973. I had been praying and I told the girls to do the same thing, and it was as if God had answered our prayers. When he came back home, two days after the coup, he was a different man. He started to become more domestic; he was even affectionate. I don't think it was just the curfew, although that did make it possible for me to watch him and keep him away from his sidekicks; rather it was the general healing brought about in the moral climate of the country as a whole. The example of corruption offered by those at the top had come to an end, and the ones who had supported the destruction of the family, of my family, had run away like rats or were in prison. His lovers were now far away, sheltered in some embassy, begging to be allowed to leave the country to continue their "activities" abroad.

Naturally, I was still suspicious, because the change had been very sudden, from one day to the next. I still remember what he told me when he came home that day. Old darling, he said to me, and he embraced me, I'm through with politics. I'm not going to be anybody's pawn again.

And ever since then he really has been a different person. He stopped seeing his old friends, he burned some documents that he had, and he has led an irreproachable life. Furthermore, his conduct enabled me to intervene personally on his behalf, so that he wouldn't lose his job, even though by all rights he should have been demoted and placed under close observation. *Señora,* I was told by the colonel with whom I spoke in the ministry, I believe everything you say, but I believe nothing he says. Your word is enough for me, *señora.* But if that scoundrel of a husband of yours goes back to his old ways, you just let me know. Because we're used to dealing with difficult people and we intend to have a little order here.

It made me sad to hear him called a scoundrel like that, but, after all, he had asked for it, running around in such bad company.

Anyway, there was no need to inform the colonel of anything. Or, at least, so I thought until yesterday. But yesterday, the unlucky thirteenth, I had a sad awakening; yesterday was the darkest and vilest day of my life and I'll always mark it on the calendar with black ink.

By chance I had to visit a sick friend who was just arriving from Concepción. The house where she would be staying was unfamiliar to me, as was the neighborhood. If I mention this seemingly insignificant detail, it's because my husband would never have suspected that I would be over in that area. You can imagine my surprise, when from the bus on which I was riding I saw my husband in person, waiting at one of the bus stops. He had the same briefcase he always carried and a record under his arm. I was even thinking about getting off the bus and greeting him, when at that very moment a young thing came up to him, planted a kiss on his cheek and took his arm as though she had known him for years. He seemed to be a bit surprised by her effusiveness, but they soon started walking off together, as happy as you please. As you can imagine, Rosalyn, I didn't waste any time. I got off the bus at the next stop and waited for them around the corner. They didn't see me, I don't know if it was because I was well hidden or because they were so absorbed in each other, talking up a storm. I was trembling with rage. I had never had any proof of his infidelity. Now I had it. I supposed that they would enter one of the nearby buildings before long, but that wasn't the case. They only stopped once, and I saw my fresh husband take something out of his brief-case. It was a gift, or at least it was gift-wrapped, and it was rather large. I have no idea what it might have contained, because she didn't seem to give it any importance and didn't open it. There went our household money. Spent for chocolates, nighties, or who knows what.

They continued walking down unfamiliar streets. They entered a café and were there for a good while. I waited outside. I kept glancing at my watch, because it was lunchtime and I knew my husband had to go back to work and downtown was a good distance away. I was hoping to be able to follow their trail to their hideaway, in order to burst in and raise a ruckus right there, catching them in the act. But they separated with a kiss, each one going his own way. I didn't know what to do, but since I had no doubt about where my shameless husband was going, I decided to follow her. A few blocks away she got into a small car and took off. As for me, I couldn't catch a cab, so I had to be satisfied with taking down her tag number, just in case.

I remained alone on that street I had never seen before and that I hoped I would never see again. I felt all the rage I had been building up for years mounting within me, a veritable fever that I couldn't control. I tortured myself thinking that I should have faced them right there, in the middle of the café, so that all the customers would witness it. But there was no proof and I have a terrible fear of looking foolish. Nonetheless, my heart was a shambles. When a woman knows something, it's because we really do know. It doesn't matter if there's evidence. The worst thing was that I had believed all his lies, I had really believed that he had changed. I felt used.

Now, Rosalyn, I don't know where to turn. That miserable excuse of a man is the father of my children. I'm joined to him by both divine and human bonds. I have loved him passionately; I've been a mother, a sister and a wife to him. Even though that love has evaporated now, even though I can't even stand to see his hypocritical face, I still can't forget that it's my duty not to separate from him as long as there's any way to repair the marriage.

Last night, when he came through the door, playing the part of the saint, and started praising the Junta's economic policies to the skies, saying that in spite of the difficulties we were going to come through it, I felt like shouting at him to shut up, shut up, shut up, three times, as loud as I could. I no longer believe anything he says, and that's the worst thing that can happen between a man and a woman.

The neighbor that I mentioned to you, who is very understanding and has lots of experience, with all the things he's done, told me— yes, I had to tell somebody; I couldn't keep that secret inside me, I would have burst—that he would talk to my husband, tell him exactly how things were. He said that it was the limit when this sort of thing happened to a fine woman like me, and that I deserved better. I admit that the tears flowed at that point, just to see that at least there was somebody in this world who recognized and appreciated my virtues. In any case, I turned down his offer, because I won't have two men fighting in my home, we've had enough with all our past divisions.

I lay awake all night with my eyes open, listening to him there beside me, sleeping like a log, as though nothing had happened. At one point I turned on the light to look at him. He looked so innocent. I wanted to press my lips to his, in a kind of farewell kiss. But I didn't do anything. I went on like that for a good while, waiting for someone to come and solve my terrible problem, waiting for him to wake up and explain that it was all a mistake, that I was the only woman in his life and his only concern. But after a while I lost all hope. It's useless to hope that a cancerous tumor will heal one day on its own. I turned off the light and the only thing I thought about, listening to his breathing, and I thought it over and over again, was that this is the man to whom I'm joined until death do us part, until death do us part.

As soon as he had left in the morning and the children had gone to school, I started writing you this letter, that I now send you hoping that some miracle will save me, that you will be able to see more clearly than I in all this darkness, because if someone doesn't help me, I don't know what I might not do.

Distraught Patriot

April 18, 1974

Dear Friend:

As you will have seen in today's issue of the newspaper, we were not able to publish your anguished letter. At any rate, I am writing to you personally, because of the importance of your particular case.

I understand your feelings, although you mustn't let yourself be carried away by despair. In the first place, you have no definite proof of your husband's misconduct. Appearances are often deceptive, especially when there have been bad experiences in the past. But one must never discount other possible explanations, even when it's natural for a woman, as prone to jealousy as anyone else, to torture herself with such suspicions.

I suggest that you watch your husband closely for the next several days, *without his realizing it*. It is precisely for that reason that we chose not to make your letter known—so that neither he nor his girlfriend nor any other acquaintance might be made aware of the situation. Treat him as usual, as difficult as that may be. When you have more substantial evidence, come to my office at the newspaper so that we can talk the matter over, woman to woman. Or, if you prefer, I can visit you personally, since you were kind enough to include your address in a postscript, along with the tag number of that young woman whom you suspect.

Underneath it all, what concerns me in your letter is something else. I detect, near the end, a frankly bitter and disillusioned tone.

You are a Christian and you cannot indulge yourself in the luxury of losing your faith in God. The Lord has ways of bringing His purposes to a good end; He has instruments, both secret and public, to carry out His will; He intervenes suddenly and drastically in the lives of evil men. Chile's recent history confirms that. I am certain that God will find a way to answer your renewed faith. As I said in my column today: you are not as abandoned or alone as you seem to believe. Hold on to your faith, and don't be surprised if the solution to your dilemma is just around the corner. Best wishes.

Rosalyn

CONSULTATION

"I'm tired," that voice says. "That's enough for now . . . How about bringing me a cup of tea?"

"With toast and cake, Lieutenant, sir?"

You note a slight hesitation in the voice, a rather long pause. You've become accustomed to measuring those pauses, those hesitations, and to interpreting them.

"With everything," that voice finally replies.

"What about this asshole, Lieutenant, sir?"

There's no hesitation now; yes to the cookies, yes to the cake, but for you not the remotest shadow of a doubt.

"Just leave him tied up. Just because I'm tired now doesn't mean this son of a bitch should be tired, right? Or are you tired, asshole? Want us to let you go now?"

You don't answer. Sometimes that works. At this point you hope that it's one of those questions that don't require an immediate answer, that it's just one more exercise. That's the way it turns out. The minutes pass. The only thing you can hear is the sound of boots slipping off and dropping to the floor, and then feet dropping heavily on the nearby table that serves as a desk, and finally an expression of satisfaction, somewhere between a sigh and a grunt. The soldiers must have sat down, too; nobody is saying anything. Then, the sharp scratch of a match, a cigarette being lit, its aroma spreading, a mild tickle of smoke visiting you. You're surprised that you have no desire to smoke. The mere idea claws at your throat and fills you with nausea. It must be your obsessive, overwhelming thirst: your body can't crave anything other than water.

Now they are bringing in a tray. You hear them taking their seats around the table, the dragging of chairs, the shuffle of papers being pushed aside and murmurings of anticipation and camaraderie.

All of a sudden, with no warning, that voice speaks to you.

"You know, Giorgio," says the voice, "you know, I have a problem." You wait for him to go on. You thought that at least during this brief period all their thoughts would focus on the food and they'd leave you in peace. "I really do have a problem. Know what it is?" Another pause. "Tell me something, Giorgio. Do you think this stuff is fattening?"

"What is it?" You hear your own voice, hoarse, as if it belonged to someone else; you're astonished at how you've managed to conserve the matter-of-fact tone of a doctor, that slightly superior questioning air, despite your hoarseness.

"A cup of tea."

"That's not fattening," you say, dryly, choosing your words with a surgeon's precision, caring for and nurturing the exchange of words, sniffing out any unexpected opening. "Unless you add a lot of sugar."

"What about the cake and the toast and butter?"

"What else?" you ask, seeing those foods parade by your blindfolded eyes, as though someone were projecting them in Technicolor on a screen; they appear momentarily, then disappear. They are as unreal as Woody Woodpecker or John Wayne, TV stars, cake, toast, butter, cheese; it's been months since you've had any of them; anything like that is beyond your wildest dreams now.

"Jelly," the voice says. "Do you think all that will make me fat?"

"What time is it?" you inquire, with an astuteness that amazes even you.

The lieutenant offers you that valuable, orienting, compass-like information with no problem.

"Five in the afternoon, Giorgio. Snack time."

Nine hours here. You would have sworn that it had been one hour or four hundred, but nine seems like an improbable number.

"For somebody who's trying to lose weight," you declare, "that's a lot for a snack. Tea, without sugar, and a few soda crackers, should be more than sufficient. And if you could cut out snacks altogether and hold out until mealtime, it would be better still."

For a while he says nothing else. They are eating, the four of them have sat down and are drinking tea, you can hear the knives scraping the burned toast, even the clicking of teeth, the chewing, someone asking for a piece of cheese.

"Listen, Giorgio, you know something?" His mouth is full but he manages to enunciate each syllable clearly. "You know you could help me out . . . You could give me a medical examination, prescribe some pills, a diet or something . . ."

"If you get me out of this position, I could." You realize it's a mistake, an incredibly stupid mistake. No doctor would stoop to beg one of his patients. There's no doubt that that one sentence can destroy the relationship you have been absurdly building up over the last few moments. But you can't help it. The pain from your wrists, tied behind the horse, from your body which is stretched to the maximum, from all the burns, is just too great. The only thing you can think about is being released and having a drink of water, if you could only have one little glass of water.

The reaction is precisely the one you feared.

"The asshole wants to leave. He wants to go already. No, my man, what you did is a serious matter, you and the other little doctors, interfering where you had no business, and now you want to get away with it. It's not that easy. You can't go around organizing clandestine hospitals and then the next day pretend it didn't happen, we'll have none of those games here." But you sense that his jaw must be more relaxed, that his fury has diminished; he hasn't stood up and walked toward you; he's still at the table and hasn't stopped eating.

"I've already explained to you." You are speaking, stubbornly, with the same obstinacy you expressed at eight o'clock this morning, when they had just brought you in. "I didn't do any of that, sir. There weren't any hospitals like the ones you talk about."

"So I'm lying, am I, asshole? Are you calling me a liar?"

"No, sir."

"Then you must be the liar, you son of a bitch. Understand?"

"Yes, sir."

Nevertheless, you sense that he's going back to the theme of food and diet, that this interests him more than supposedly clandestine hospitals and the stocking of food for a civil war that was never fought and the secret wards for the wounded and the poisoning of wells in the wealthy neighborhoods and all the other stupid accusations.

"You know all about this kind of thing, right?" asks the lieutenant's voice. "This nutrition business, I mean."

"It's very difficult to talk under these conditions, Lieutenant," you tell him.

He laughs. "I guess you really aren't very comfortable, are you? It's not exactly like your office, shall we say. Okay, okay, you win, asshole. Untie him. Untie Giorgio for me."

When they've undone the last knot, you collapse on the floor in a bundle. You try to stand up, but you have no control over your arms and legs. You remain in that position, in a heap, still unable to enjoy the relief of muscles that no longer have to contract before the next blow, unable to believe that they've finally removed you from the bars of the horse. You can feel your own breathing against your face and the beating of your heart, bigger than your whole body, as it echoes within you, saturating you, running over.

"Stand him there," the lieutenant says.

Two pairs of hands lift you up forcefully.

"Shit, he's a heavy son of a bitch, Lieutenant," one of the soldiers says.

"Big and dumb," the other one assents. "He's the king-size variety."

"Less complaining and more work," cuts in the voice of the lieutenant. "The asshole's not so big. He ought to be about our size now. That's why we've been softening him up all day . . . Isn't that right, Giorgio?"

You choose to remain silent, hope that he doesn't insist, but this time the officer expects an answer and he repeats the question, so you are obliged to answer, "Yes, that's right, sir, all day." They put you on a cot. It must be in one corner of the room, because there seems to be less light.

"Okay, Giorgio, ready? You're as free as a bird. We're treating you like a prince, Giorgio, that's all I've got to say . . . Would you like something else, or are you happy now?"

You dare to ask for a little water.

The lieutenant is shocked. You sense the hardening, the suspicion, the distrust that return to his throat like some reptile.

"Forget the water, okay? A lot of assholes have died on us 'cause we gave them water. You have to wait at least three hours for water, after the electricity."

"The water killed them?" There's real curiosity in your question, you sense your own mind calculating, wondering, classifying.

"They drink water and croak, just like that. So we've cut out the water . . . Don't try to kill yourself on me, Giorgio, you hear? We've still got a lot of talking to do."

"That has no scientific foundation whatsoever," you suggest, injecting your professorial tone with all the certainty you can manage.

"Don't come to me with that story," the lieutenant announces. "I've seen it with my own eyes. You barely give them a little water, and *ciao,* bye-bye, off they go."

"It had to be something else, Lieutenant. I can assure you it had nothing to do with any physiological phenomenon."

There's a pause. You can hear the lieutenant getting up from the table and walking toward the cot. He's walking without his boots on. When he speaks, he's practically on top of you.

"You're really thirsty, huh, Giorgio? That's why you don't care about dying."

"I'm really thirsty," you affirm. "But I'm not talking about that now. What you propose is biologically impossible. Water can't harm an organism that's been affected by electricity."

"What about when an electrical appliance falls into the bathtub?"

You permit a slight note of impatience to invade your words. "That's an entirely different matter. Water is a conductor of electricity, but I'm talking about water that you drink, not about being immersed in water."

The lieutenant talks, as if to himself.

"And all those assholes that croaked. What do you think of that . . . Their hearts just stop, Giorgio, they just stop working, that's all."

"Have there been many?" you ask, trying to hide your emotion, attempting to make any note of doubt purely academic.

"Quite a few," says the lieutenant.

"Cardiac arrest has lots of causes," you pronounce, "but ingesting water isn't one of them."

"Okay. You've convinced me," says the lieutenant. "Go get the doctor some water . . . But, I'm warning you, Giorgio. If you kick off, you're responsible. Understand? Don't say I didn't warn you. I wash my hands of the whole matter if something happens."

You don't reply and he goes back to the table. He asks you to prescribe a moderate diet for him. You ask him his age, his weight, his height. He gives you all the information without the least suspicion, with no thought that he's providing you with clues to his identity. You tell him that it would have been better for you to have examined him, to have known more about his medical history, but that, anyway, you can advise him as to some basic measures to take. He writes down everything in order, repeating your instructions in a low voice, undoubtedly using the same pencil and paper he has been using to take down your statement. You suggest that to provide any more detail you would need greater serenity, and that he should consult you tomorrow.

He must be reading your curriculum vitae now, because he murmurs the names of some foreign universities, conferences, publications, as though confirming and reiterating your qualifications in that area.

"Listen, Giorgio," he says all of a sudden. "How did somebody like you get involved with assholes like these?" You don't answer. You concentrate on the water that's taking so long to get here, on the fact that it's five in the afternoon and that with any luck at all today's session has come to an end. "Aren't you ashamed to go around with these criminals? I mean, you're tops in your field, you know, why screw it up and waste your time with all those nobodies?"

You wait a moment, gather up your strength; you're about to speak again, to explain what the Allende government was all about, not only in the area of health care, but for the country as a whole; you think that it's always better to make things clear again and again, something has to remain, to keep on stirring, some echo should resound into the future, but the lieutenant prevents your speaking by asking another question.

"Hey, Giorgio," and now there is something definitively strange in the outlines of his voice, something soft and gentle in his diction. "It says here you don't have any kids. Is that right?"

"In fact, it is," you answer, noting that behind the blindfold your eyes half-close.

"Why's that?" the lieutenant asks. "How come you never thought of having kids?"

For a second time you hear your own words as if they come from a stranger, the same words you've pronounced on other occasions, at parties, in the office, at dinners, but that you never expected to have to repeat here, in this cellar or barracks or whatever it is: "We didn't have any, we couldn't have any," you hear yourself saying.

"But there are scientific ways to fix that." You hear the lieutenant stop talking. He approaches, but not as close as the previous time. "My wife and I had that problem, too, Giorgio . . . But now everything has turned out okay. I was sure it had nothing to do with me. That's what I told the doctor . . . Now we just have to wait three months for the little guy; he'll be born this fall. What do you think of that?"

"Congratulations," you say, with no irony in your voice. "Your wife must be very happy."

"The whole thing was damned expensive," the voice replies, "but it's worth it, I can tell you it's really worth it . . . If you want, I'll recommend you to the doctor. He's at the Military Hospital, over there by Los Leones, you know?"

You choose your words carefully. "No, thank you, lieutenant. We've already tried. It makes no sense to keep on."

At that moment, they bring you the water. A hand lifts your head and you drink slowly, feeling its coolness sparkle in your mouth and on your tongue and down your throat. Flowing between your gums as along a dry riverbed, the water comforts and brightens the rest of your body, like some second blood supply, transparent and sacred. Only after you have emptied that glass and another do you realize that the lieutenant and the other soldiers have been observing you closely, anxiously waiting for your heart to stop beating then and there, expecting the onset of palpitations and then your demise right before their eyes. But nothing happens. You feel your convulsed limbs relaxing, even the burns seem to pain you less, the water has cooled and refreshed you down to the bottoms of your feet, even your brain seems to work better.

"How do you like that! And all those assholes that croaked from the water!" the lieutenant says, possibly shaking his head in astonishment. "And in the first session, without our getting a thing out of them, not even a little signature. They just drank the water and that was that, *ciao,* bye-bye."

"It wasn't the water, Lieutenant." You raise your voice angrily. "What happens is that you people get carried away. Then you blame the water."

"You're real smart, Giorgio," the voice says. "You think that you'll get us to go easier that way, that we'll relax the pressure. No, sir, forget that. We have a duty to fulfill and we're going to see it through, yes, sir. We're going to keep on doing it."

"And they're going to keep on dying on you," you warn, putting all the necessary conviction in the balance.

"Better dead than silent," says the lieutenant, moving away toward the table. "Okay. Take these things away. No more cake from now on, understand. Just soda crackers or water crackers. Which ones are better anyway, Giorgio, soda crackers or water crackers?"

"It makes no difference," you say. "The main thing is to do away with the bread and jam."

"I'll tell you, doctor, I'll tell you what we're going to do . . . When you're free, when you've confessed everything and we release you, I'm going to send for you. Don't worry—we'll let you relax for a few days. Then we'll send for you. A chauffeured limousine right to your door. You still live in the same place, don't you?"

"Yes," you say.

"We'll have a few friendly drinks at the Military Club. We'll have a nice little chat. We'll come to an agreement. Then we'll go see my son. I don't live far from there. We'll go see him so you can give him a little examination . . . because what I really want is for you to be my little boy's doctor. How's that?"

You say nothing.

"We're the ones in charge of this country now," the voice goes on. "And we deserve the best doctors."

"I have to pee," you say suddenly.

"Besides," the voice adds, "before long they're going to promote me to captain."

"Have to pee," you insist, "I have to pee."

"Take him," the lieutenant orders. "And treat the doctor gently, okay? Don't let him fall apart on the way."

Once again you feel those two pairs of hands under your arms, fingernails that dig into and scratch your skin, you know you're falling and that they can barely hold you up. Your legs and feet are like dead weight and they have to drag you out of the room, toward the toilet, along a passageway that is suddenly dark and cold. You're naked, so they won't have to unfasten anything, they don't even have to undress you, your own modesty astonishes you.

"Here we are," the one on your right explains.

"Lift the blindfold a little, so I can see," you say, worried about peeing on yourself, but they don't answer, they don't pay you any mind.

"Just go on and piss, doctor," the same one says.

But now it doesn't want to come out. You can sense the nearby chill of the tiles, the sour smell of dampness, defecation, and confinement, and the sturdy hands that hold you up and watch you. It's as though they had cut off your genitals, as if there were nothing but a great, empty, absent hole hanging between your legs.

"You know, doctor," the same voice says all of a sudden. "I've got a problem, too." You let him continue, you try to immerse yourself in the need to urinate, to expel everything that's swelling you up inside and that only a few moments ago was about to explode violently. "You know, doctor, I stayed small. They call me Tiny—that's what they call me. You think there's any remedy that'll make me grow, doctor?"

And now, finally, the pee does start to itch and burn and to flow, like a hose that explodes, maybe it splatters your legs, your lungs breathe as if your bladder had been a pestilential balloon on the point of bursting. You're grateful for these small gifts, these tiny victories, a glass of water, some knots that are untied, urine that is no longer blocked, a heart that amazingly goes on beating, the wonder of a conscience that knows no confusion nor betrayal.

"Doctor?"

"How old are you?" And the only thing that hammers away at you is the desire to cover yourself, even if it's just a pair of shorts, just some pants to cover you, a blanket over your legs, over your shoulders.

"Eighteen, doctor. Is it too late now?"

"I'd have to see an X-ray of your hand. I can't make any promises."

"Thanks, doctor."

"Have your hand X-rayed, either one, and send me the X-ray. I'll give you the address. Maybe we can work out something."

"Thanks, doctor."

On the way back you'd like to no longer be a dead weight on the shoulders of the two men; you'd like to avoid the role of invalid or baby or drunk; you try to anchor your leg that is floating somewhere down there at an unreachable distance, and the little needles of pain climbing and biting at the inside of your thigh are the ambiguous joy of your own existence; now the whole thigh, your groin, with a note of familiarity in the cold that cramps your muscles, and now another step, just to be able to face the lieutenant without swaying on the shoulders of the two soldiers, out of one corner of the blindfold you can glimpse the consternation of your own naked foot, far away, slowly advancing, limping along the corridor, you can hardly believe that's really your foot, and now everything's going better, you're almost walking, groping, guided by the two boys at your sides, until you finally reach what must be the threshold of that room and you grow tense, the soldiers must notice that involuntary stiffening: in the murmur of voices that reach the three of you, a different accent can be distinguished, someone who has not been there during the previous hours, the harshness of a new voice.

"Oh, Giorgio," the lieutenant says, "I'm glad you're back, very kind of you. I was just talking to the colonel about what you told us about the water. I was telling him that your scientific and medical knowledge has really amazed us. Isn't that right, Colonel? Isn't that what we were saying?"

The other man does not answer.

This time they don't take you to the cot. They stand you in front of the table where the two officers are surely seated, and there they support your weight for a while as if they were presenting you for inspection at a college or boarding school, as though you were hanging in a butcher-shop window. You try to stand straight, to plant both feet firmly on the floor, but you know that if they let you go, you won't be able to stay on your feet.

"Look, Giorgio," the lieutenant's voice goes on. "I was just explaining this medical problem to the colonel. Colonel, do you remember that just the day before yesterday I was assuring you that it wasn't our fault that we lost a few of them? Remember? We need consultation; that's what we need. According to the doctor here, we get carried away sometimes. We just don't realize how weak these civilians are. If you had just been here, Colonel. If you'd only heard the advice Giorgio here gave us, the things he knows. With a specialist like him, we wouldn't lose another one."

You now hear that deep, solemn, gravelly voice you haven't heard all day, that sharp, new voice, the colonel's.

"That's fine, Lieutenant. After all, you're not asking for anything extraordinary . . . I imagine we wouldn't have any trouble finding some of the doctors' colleagues in Santiago who would be willing to collaborate with the authorities. What do you think, doctor?"

You choose to remain silent, to blot out those dizzying voices. But at that moment the lieutenant must have made some silent signal to the two soldiers, because they release you, leaving you there, in front of the table, unattached. All of a sudden it's as if a window had opened in the floor at your feet, you try to stand alone, a wave of vertigo strikes you and blows on you from every direction, there's no use begging the shit that was your legs to obey you while you vainly wait, as you fall, for a lightning flash of hands to appear miraculously and grab you so you won't collapse, at least Tiny's hands, the minuscule hands of the soldier who didn't grow, the hands that would have to be X-rayed to see if the metacarpal bones had stopped growing, but there's nothing there, no one, you are lucky enough to fall on your shoulder, to not hit your head like the last time.

"They may not have the quality of Giorgio here," the lieutenant says, standing up from the table, pushing his chair back, approaching you. "They may not have his credentials, but we have to work with what we have." You feel the lieutenant's foot pushing at your stomach lazily, almost like some familiar yet irritating caress. You can see the toe of a long and shiny boot from under your hood. When did he put the boots on again? You do not have the time to be mildly surprised that this is the question that comes to your mind. "We can't allow the patients to go on dying on us like that.

So we're going to talk about that tomorrow, aren't we, Giorgio? We still have lots of interesting things to talk about. Listen, I'm talking to you, asshole. Speak up when I'm talking to you, do you hear?"

You don't say anything. Under the hood you close your eyes in order not to see that boot and you wait for the second kick.

TRADEMARK TERRITORY

Chile:
25% unemployment.

Official Statistics

. . . and then the door bursts open as if driven by a gust of wind and he comes in, embracing her and tossing the kids in the air and laughing, happy for the first time in eight months, feeling like the man of the house again, the one who brings home the bacon, the breadwinner, and, well, old girl, I got a job, they hired me, they hired me and tomorrow I have a training course all day, then on Thursday I'm on my own, I'll be a salesman, selling the latest thing, so she should go to Don Fernando's store and ask him to trust us one more time, to tell him I have a contract now, that it's a sure thing, I'll earn a ten percent commission on sales and those appliances sell like hotcakes, and we need some rice, a few onions, flour, eggs, a little milk for the kids . . .

Congratulations. You've been chosen from among fifty thousand applicants to fill eight vacancies as doorbell salesmen. You will see, as this course proceeds, that we're dealing with a very special bell, patented and sold only by Health and Home, our company, a bell which screens visitors to the home. Now, a small demonstration. Do we have a volunteer? Thank you. Let's bring that warm finger closer, that sweaty palm, this way, yes, that's it, you're going to press the product in question with the obvious intention of ultimately getting into that home. The bell responds to this pressure in one of two different ways. The first and normal response is for the bell to sound, so that the residents of the house can be advised of the presence of a friend and thus welcome him. The second response—and this is the characteristic that distinguishes our product from all others on the market—is for the bell to reject the request of the caller. It does so by means of a slight electrical reaction, like this, just like this, thank you, Mr. Salesman, for graciously lending us your finger for this demonstration, you can return to your seat now, there's no permanent damage to the brain, just a slight spasm of the skin, but we've already administered a corrective for this unfortunate individual. Please write down in your notes that that electrical charge is authorized by the Interior Ministry and supervised by the Ministry of Energy and Commerce, and is purely pedagogical in nature. It is administered only if the bell perceives excessive timidity in the finger that touches it. In which case it will automatically block the entry of any young man with a slightly frayed collar and tie who might come forward to offer his services, whether to wash windows, walk the dog, rake the leaves, whatever the case may be, madam, sir, miss, at your service. The mechanism is equipped with a magical nose that will immediately pick up from that hand any sign of excessive, albeit disguised, hunger, will sniff out any foot odor at that early hour of the day. The caller has smelly feet! What greater proof do you need to confirm that those limbs have already covered many city blocks in search of a few crumbs of bread, weighed down by empty bottles for babies whose hunger is never satisfied, that those feet have already paraded their poverty in front of downtown shops, dreaming in front of the windows, that they've dragged themselves to and from ever more distant towns, because they can no longer afford the bus fare? The bell is infallible; in accordance with scientific laws, it has determined that this same young man today will bother not only this home but many others as well. Which, as stated clearly in Article 84 of the new labor code—be sure to memorize that paragraph!—gives you the right to penalize the beggar, petitioner, job seeker and good-for-nothing who turns up to annoy the mistress of the house in the middle of her morning chores, just when she's writing the day's menu for the cook and going over the chauffeur's accounts. That's what the bell is for, to keep everything in its proper place, meting out tiny, almost painless jolts, educational buzzes. It's now nine in the morning and someone will surely appear with the same old song and dance: Would you have some old clothes, ma'am? Some floors that need waxing? Perhaps your children need tutoring in piano, or English, or botany or maybe trigonometry? Let's understand that we're often dealing with very well-spoken people, in fact, even well-shod, and with a certain level of culture. No one can affirm that they're delinquents just because they're unemployed. But any excessive excitement or anxiety flowing from the fingertips, any annoying hoarseness tickling the throat, is enough to activate the bell implacably. It knows how to separate the wheat from the chaff, this bell, it knows family friends like the back of its hand and the door is opened automatically to trustworthy people, even before they get there, it welcomes them with the triumphal music of Lully. This product has pedigree. It knows that at ten in the morning homeowners do not want their view sullied. So your morning exercises and your Japanese flower petal sauna won't be interrupted by the downstairs maid, coming and going with useless and unfailingly boring messages, the reply to which must inevitably be negative. You have to save those lips; it's not good to waste your vocal cords with useless repetitions. Let's not have an impertinent bell ringing in the middle of the morning, just when little Richie is playing in the pool and about to swim his first stroke and the Instamatic camera goes click. Let the bell answer for the lady of the house while she tastes the Coquilles Saint-Jacques and puts them back in the oven to glaze while she awaits the arrival of the gentleman of the house for lunch. Don't forget these examples, because they constitute true psychological motivations for buying the product; they show that you respect your patrons' lives and customs. Remember that our product is trained to sense that undeniable aura of defensiveness which the poor wear like a cloak, when they appear at the door to sell forks, shawls, spoons, chairs, and all of it at the precise hour that the family is sitting down for lunch. The X-ray and infrared mechanisms in the bell are sensitized to distinguish the worn article of clothing, the frayed elbow, the tie that just doesn't match the socks, the eyeglasses that are being held together by a paper clip. At this point, nonetheless, you have to allay certain doubts of the young people of the house. This mechanism can in no way, you will say, block the entry of those who are wearing worn-out jeans or to those who have multicolored patches on their lovely garb. Perish the thought! The Bell is aware of the latest advances in style, it has real swing, not to mention punch. It's easy to prove that it's a prototype for fanatical ecologists, master conserver of energy in these times of petroleum crises, with an internal thermostat that limits and regulates the level of its charge capacity.

Its magnetic memory recognizes the repeat offender, the one who shows up again months later to ring the same bell to sell the same soup bowl or the same set of mock china. A double dose, one for being unworthy to touch that button even once, and the second for being an amnesiac idiot on top of it, so that this little scorching will be the last one and it won't have to be increased yet more, the third and final time, when the solicitor is fried. That's the way people learn: that scorched forefinger will be a reminder and a guide for the rest of his life. Be careful. For those purchasers who may be upset by violence, now is the time to insist that it's not a matter of isolating the family from the stir of outside life, which really should be introduced into the bosom of every home that considers itself modern. This bell, ladies and gentlemen, is capable of selecting a couple of beggars each month to whom you could donate that pair of old slippers that are no longer of any use to you, or how about a little bread, my good man, a few leftovers from our dinner two nights ago? The instrument possesses the necessary magnanimity to allow those grimy fingers, smelling of grease and soot, of weakness and suffering, to touch its august face, the immaculate surface of this Prince of Butlers. When you offer this product, my young aspiring salesman, you must emphasize its common sense, its protective but not isolating benefits, which allow a reasonable quota of indigents to get through so that their hosts can show their charitable nature. In these times when it's the in-thing for the housewife to sell raffle tickets to benefit the orphans at her afternoon bridge teas, we guarantee that this bell can sched-ule regular incursions from the outside world. It therefore pos-sesses an innate sense of the dramatic. What could be more appropriate, in the middle of the most heated after-dinner marital spat, than the sound of the front door bell to divert attention from the subject, to calm spirits and to allow the appearance of a starving stranger to reconcile the husband and wife? Being respectful of the family's privacy, it can also spice up life with the seething, passionate, obscure existence of those who suffer from powerful emotions and moving personal tragedies. Programmed by distin-guished psychiatrists, the Bell digs into the preferences and ap-petites of its clients. And you, my dear aspirants, can know no less than the product you are offering: you must master that same art of stimulating those interests, of appealing to every whim of the

customer's personality. The moment has come to place on the table
not only the Model itself, but also extensive additional equipment,
accompanied by catalogues. This one, madam, leaves whip marks,
that one, on the other hand, is called the Hemlock Model, it bites
the persistent not on the finger but on the tongue, while this other
one twists the arm of anyone who dares put on rubber gloves to
avoid the electric shock. And here, sir, we have a magnificent
example of the Slap in the Face Model, an amazing innovation.
You have to lay out all this additional material when the lady of
the house begins to hesitate, when she's looking for other benefits.
That's when you have to toy with her superiority complex: we're
not talking about cheap merchandise; the home is not losing a
beggar, it's gaining a friend, a real son. It's a privilege to own this
product, we don't offer it to just anybody. This Bell marks the
dividing line between the Yes, of Course group and the Forget It
group, between those who have the right to date your daughter
and those who shouldn't get anywhere near her. Then, to drive it
all home, you dramatize, in the customer's presence, various typical
situations: Tell the lady of the house I'm prepared to repair any
plumbing problem she might have, I'm a certified mechanic, en-
gineer, nuclear scientist, you know, ma'am, with the present unemployment rate, tell her I have a great voice and I'll give singing
lessons in exchange for a dish of beans every two weeks, ask the
lady if she'd like to buy combs, goat cheese, little plastic toy cars,
colonial lighting fixtures. Make the customer nervous with all those
threats of possible intrusions. And at that point the Bell itself
appears, like a busload of soldiers, like a gentle and silent volley
of machine-gun fire, the Bell sniffs and smells the air around the
offending finger, and almost, only almost, we don't promise miracles, it almost doesn't need to feel the tips of the fingers on the
button, it's enough for the intruder to get close to produce a
reaction, it's enough for it to realize that he's coming to beg, to
offer, to plead, to harass, he doesn't have any work and it's now
four in the afternoon, and he hasn't eaten a mouthful all day, not
even breakfast, and he has the nerve to put his finger on a Piece
of Merchandise of that caliber. And nobody tricks it with good
manners and gallant gestures, it isn't taken in by poems by Gabriela
Mistral about children's games, or by snapshots of a deaf-mute
brother who needs an operation. None of that business. Its judg-

ments are without appeal for those who come without letters of recommendation: this guy lost his job eight months ago, this one here lost his a year ago, this other one lost his kid because he couldn't afford a doctor, this one can't even get it up in bed anymore, and this one would be willing to lick the toilet clear with his tongue for a pot of veggies, and this one has gums like mashed pasta. All callers are fed into the Bell's computer. It knows how to disconnect those ungrateful voices so they won't be heard inside: I'm an architect, ma'am, don't you want me to build you a birdhouse; I'm a gardener, ma'am, can't I pull your weeds; I'm a nurse, ma'am, I can give your cat a shot. That's what Mr. Bell is all about, His Excellency the Threshold, His Doormanship, Sir Electricity, so show some enthusiasm, boys, the customer always likes that. And that warm little electrode pricks the overeager finger, terrorizes the tissues, interrupts the breathing for a few seconds, leaving the intrusive bodies with that same sensation of painful numbness that our volunteer saleman has just experienced, in the pit of his stomach, in the passageway of the penis, in the creaking of a vertebra. Let them know they can't bother us just like that at six in the evening when the gentleman of the house is approaching the liquor cabinet to choose tonight's cocktail, we can't receive anyone now, don't insist, come back next week, the year before last, we already have someone to take care of the chrysanthemums, where's your sense of dignity, man, are you some kind of whore, young woman, offering yourself like this from house to house, decent people don't go around soliciting employment from complete strangers, where are your credentials, your visiting card? The Bell fixes its searching eye on any shadow that crowds the doorway at eight in the evening, while the family is having dinner together. Our Bell who art at the door, at the windows, at the drawbridges, at the control towers, hallowed be Thy Buzz, Bell who knows how to distinguish the wealthy from the mendicant, Bell who allows us to enjoy our daily hors d'oeuvre, Bell who answers our prayers down to the final letter, and who never indulges in cheap sentimentality, our Lord the Bell, who has never left a man crippled or mute or paralyzed, although our unscrupulous competitors would accuse us of every kind of infraction just to lower our sales, Bell who only frees our thresholds of the drunk, the filthy, the unemployed, the widowed, and all those who ask God's favor or any kind of favor, who invoke your Bell in vain. Bell whose perfection is such that you even know when our windows really need washing, or our third-floor balcony needs retiling, Bell who lets only the lowest bidder pass. Learn this hymn by heart, boys, it's our company's ABC. And now, ladies and gentlemen, everyone is sleeping except the Bell, guarder of decency, the best shield against disagreeable dreams, because any nightmare that would dare appear gets electrocuted in the act, now that's a real Bell, your own private curfew, martial law made to order, that's all ready to go into action at six in the morning, prepared to scream its little warning into the first fist that comes to knock unwisely at your door a little before eight, protector of your daughter's purity, of your ancestors' peaceful tombs, of all the portraits on your family tree, so now the clock has gone its full circle, twenty-four hours in the life of a Bell, every minute of dedicated service, if there were such an instrument in every well-to-do home in the country, we would have no more problems of delinquency, vagrancy, our economy would be under control once and for all, there'd be an end to this plague of beggars that won't let us live in peace. And once every household here is equipped, why not really mass-produce the product, for exportation, gentlemen? Then the sales would be enormous. A Bell in every throat.

Do you all have pamphlets? Are the instructions clear? Are you ready and willing? Fine. Good luck to each of you, the course is over.

. . . and a moment before he rings the doorbell, he seems to realize something, wants to step back; he senses something, but sees how his finger inexorably draws nearer, as if he no longer had any control over it; it will be the morning's first sale; he's too anxious, and before he touches the bell he receives that definitive cry of the flesh which leads him to clearly understand that in that house, and in the next one and the next one he is not going to be able to sell that product.

GODFATHER

For Fernando Ortiz Letelier

How far are we from harvesting the fruit? Just as the seed needs water to swell and to burst into a plant, so the blossom and the fruit need warmth in order to mature. Our hearts hold a great deal of warmth, so let's blow on the embers a little more, let's increase the heat and then the fruit will fall into our hands.

Luis Emilio Recabarren, 1917
*Father of the Chilean Workers Movement
and the Chilean Communist Party*

These words are, above all, for the poor women of this land.

Salvador Allende, last words
to the people of Chile, 1973

There was hardly anyone in line in front of the window, so she didn't have to wait that long.

"You all go sit over there, on that bench," she whispered to the children. As she noticed that the oldest was about to accompany his brothers and sisters, she held him back. "Not you, Luis. You stay here with me."

When it was her turn, she didn't say anything for a few moments, waiting for the clerk to speak. It was the same one as yesterday.

"I'm back, sir. Do you remember me?"

"What can I do for you, ma'am?"

"But I already explained. I'm here to register the child."

The clerk scrutinized her face again and seemed to recognize her. "Oh, yes, of course. The one who left her documents at home."

"You refused to register the boy," she said. "Now I have what you asked for, sir."

The clerk accepted the document she was holding out to him.

"The law is the law, ma'am. Nothing to be done. We can't do a thing without the proper documentation."

She did not answer. The child who was at her side stood on his tiptoes in order to see better. His eyes just reached the bottom of the window.

"Right, ma'am. When was the child born?"

"Eight days ago."

An expression of impatience crossed the clerk's face. "That's impossible, ma'am. The law clearly states that he must be registered within three days."

"I'm truly sorry, sir, but it was eight days ago," she said. "The fourth of November to be exact."

"This is not your first child, ma'am. By now you should know how these things are done."

"It's the first time I've done it myself, sir. If you want, I can show you the baby. I brought him along, just in case you needed to see him." She pointed vaguely in the direction of the group of children sitting with their legs dangling on the small bench against the wall of the Registry Office. The oldest, a girl, was holding the baby.

"I believe I told you yesterday that the physical presence of the subject in question is not required . . ."

"I just thought it might be necessary. I'm truly sorry, sir."

"Right, ma'am, that's all right. We'll make an exception in your case. But I must advise you that the next time you'll have to send someone else to register the child within the time allotted by the law. Do you understand?"

Something changed ever so slightly in her voice.

"I won't be having any more children, sir. This is the last one."

"Right, ma'am, that's your business. But if you do decide to have another, you've been advised. Send someone else. The father, an older brother. But someone who is not a minor, of course. It has to be an adult."

"Thank you, sir."

"Where did the birth take place, ma'am? In this district?"

She pointed toward the certificate. "At home, sir. You have the address there. It's the same."

He copied the address on a piece of paper. "Your Police Certificate, please."

"I beg your pardon?"

"The Police Certificate, ma'am. If he wasn't born at the hospital, then I must have proof of birth from the competent authority."

"But the baby is right over there, sir."

The clerk sighed. He took off his glasses and began cleaning them rapidly. He then put them on once more.

"I'm going to explain, ma'am. You must bring a small piece of paper, like this one, signed by the desk sergeant of your local police department."

"Sergeant Silva?"

"Yes, ma'am. I suppose it must be Sergeant Silva. He has to testify that the child was born on the date you say."

"But he wasn't even there. How is he going to testify?"

The clerk felt the child's black eyes staring at him. His nose wasn't visible, just that pair of dark eyes at the level of the window.

"Ma'am, I should send you back to get that certification."

"Again!"

". . . but in view of your condition and the fact that you already came yesterday, and, well, since you brought all these children, I'm going to register the baby for you and overlook the matter of the certification. But I hope you understand that all this is highly irregular."

"I'm truly sorry, sir," she said. "My husband always took care of these problems before. This is the first time for me."

"That's all right, ma'am. What's the child's name?"

The woman didn't hesitate an instant.

"Luis Emilio."

The clerk blinked. Then, pressing his lips together, he consulted the marriage record which lay on the desk in front of him, opened to the page reserved for births.

"Madam," he said finally.

"Yes, sir?"

"If I'm not mistaken, you already have a son by that name."

"Yes, sir. He's the boy who's here by my side. His name is also Luis Emilio, just like his father's, sir."

"Madam," said the clerk, "you can't give the child that name, not the new one."

"And why not? I know my rights. We're the ones responsible for having the child baptized."

The clerk noticed that a considerable line had formed and was extending itself behind her. Ostentatiously, he looked at his watch.

"I don't have all morning, ma'am. Please understand that I've agreed to register this child even though he doesn't have the proper certificates. We're doing you a very big favor. You must understand that there can't be two children in the same family with the same name. It's illegal."

"This child," she declared, "is going to have his father's name. So, you just write down Luis Emilio González Jaramillo. That's what I want."

The clerk brusquely got up from his chair, moving slightly away from the woman. He raised his voice for the first time, but not enough so that the other people in the line, all men, could hear him. "Mrs. González, you're not going to give your son that name for the simple reason that I'm not going to accept it. Not me, not anybody else in this office, not anybody in any other Registry in the country. You already have one child with that name and you can't have another. That's the law." He sat down again, somewhat calmer, took off his glasses and put them on again. "Just imagine the chaos that would result if we all had the same name."

She didn't budge from the position she had assumed, entrenched, hovering over the window. She almost erased the horizon from the clerk's view. Her every word was categorical.

"This child's father wants him to be given that name, his own name, and neither you nor I nor anyone else can prevent it. Please write it there, clearly, Luis Emilio González Jaramillo."

"Madam, this is the Department of Records. We're very busy. Why don't you ask your husband to come and register the child himself? I'm sure he would be more reasonable. Since he's already done this kind of thing . . ."

She attempted to get even closer, but it was impossible. She lowered her voice to a half-whisper.

"That's what I've been trying to explain, sir. That's why I had to come. Because he can't."

The clerk picked up the book and opened it to the first page. There was the woman's photograph, and beside it her husband's. When he looked up, he confronted the child's stare, which refused to release him. He turned his attention to the book again, and then, with a determined gesture, he closed it.

"I'm very sorry, ma'am. Truly, please believe me when I say I'm sorry . . . But there's nothing that I can do. If you're willing to give him another name, we can take care of it right now. If not, I must ask you to step aside, so that I can take care of the people who are waiting."

"Then you're not going to do me this favor, sir?"

"I've already told you, ma'am, that I can't solve your problem. Decide for yourself what to do. Next?"

She stepped to one side of the window. A man took the position that she had occupied until that moment. The woman calmly watched how the procedures were carried out for him. The small talk between the man and the clerk, the ease with which everything was completed. When the man had gone, the clerk avoided looking at her. He called for the next person in line.

She stayed there like that for a long while, watching the fathers of the children pass by, motionless, except at one moment when she took her son's hands in her own. The act of registration was a speedy process, clean, easy, and complete. The name of one child was Antonio. Another was Jorge Hugo. The one who came next was Gumercindo Sebastián. All newborn, all registered by their fathers, or in his absence, by an uncle, or, in one case, by a grand-father.

All of a sudden the clerk raised his voice louder than usual.

"The last one for this morning," his voice declared, as though announcing a train departure. "The rest of you may return this afternoon."

Her eyes rested on the shoulder of the man who was standing nearby, the gentleman who had brought all the pertinent docu-ments. When he left, she jumped quickly into his place.

"What if we put Emilio Luis?" Her voice came out in a torrent.

"Madam," he said, without raising his eyes, a mountain of fatigue in his body, his back, his neck, "why don't you just give him another name and we can take care of this once and for all? You're going to have to register the child anyhow. Why not save yourself one more day of waiting, not to mention the busfare? How about it?"

"I walked," she said.

The office was emptying. Everyone was leaving for lunch. One of the clerk's colleagues passed by.

"Hurry it up, Federico."

He said he'd be there, that they should wait for him in the casino.

"Madam, you can see, we're about to close. You can't stay here. You'll have to wait outside."

She paid no attention to him. "Can we change his name later?" she asked. "They say there's a new law, that people can take a new name."

He seemed very tired. He got up from his chair and slowly began to arrange the papers that were on the desk. There was almost no one left in the office. Another colleague was calling him from the door. He picked up a small chain, one of those they put across the window to indicate that it is closed.

She stopped him with a determined gesture.

"Don't close up on me, sir. All right. I'll give him another name . . . You'll wait on me, won't you?"

He remained standing there, quietly, with the chain still in his hand, as if he were listening to a faraway sound. The chain swung back and forth in the air. He signaled to the colleague who was still waiting at the door for him. Then he reached out his hand to receive the book for the second time that morning.

"Maruja," she called. "Bring the baby."

He still didn't sit down.

"All right," he said, picking up the pen and still holding the chain in his left hand. "What name shall we put?"

She pronounced the words serenely. "Salvador," she said. "Write down Salvador then."

He saw that the last colleague had understood and was leaving. The only one remaining in the office was a solitary janitor who, far from them, on the other side of the room, was waiting, with some impatience, for them to finish, so that he could lock the doors used by the public.

He repeated the name in a low voice.

"Sal-va-dor."

The woman took the baby in her arms and showed him to the clerk. "Salvador González Jaramillo," she explained, stopping after each syllable. "Here he is."

The children tried to climb up on the window to see how the clerk was writing the name down, skillfully and with determined precision. Only then did he hand her the book, together with a paper.

"Sign here for me," he said.

"I don't know how to write."

The clerk gave her a pen in silence. Then he declared, "That doesn't matter, madam, I assure you it doesn't matter in the least. Just make an X there, that's all, there on the dotted line, at the bottom of the page."

"I just never learned," she said. "He always took care of all these things."

The clerk took the paper with her mark.

"I don't suppose you brought a witness, did you, madam?"

"A witness?"

"The law requires that if the father doesn't register the child, the person who does should be accompanied by an adult male, preferably the nearest relative."

"I didn't bring anyone," she said, looking around her.

Once again the clerk was aware of the child's black eyes resting on him, along with the eyes of the other children, who were observing him with interest.

"Then, if you don't mind, madam," he said, "I'll sign it myself as witness."

"Thank you very much, sir. You're very kind."

"It's nothing at all. We always do it."

The clerk wrote his own name on the certificate and then signed it. He then closed the window with the chain, put a copy of the paper away, along with the pen, and then began to arrange a stack of papers carefully.

"So it's Salvador González Jaramillo," he said. "So that's the name of the little man, is it?"

The woman took the older child's face in her hands and raised it up. He had to stop staring at the clerk and to fix his big black eyes on his mother and on the baby that she was now showing him.

"Your little brother has a name now," she stated. "What do you think of that? Wouldn't Papa be pleased? Do you think he'd be pleased?"

The child returned the gaze with infinite serenity, and, swallowing deeply, he spoke for the first time that morning.

"Yes," said Luis Emilio. "Papa is going to be really happy when he comes back."

He tried out something like a small smile.

Then he sensed, guessed, knew, that behind his back, the clerk was also smiling.

TITAN

Since they were going to kill him anyhow, since tomorrow they would tell his mother the same cock-and-bull story the colonel had already told her about the death of his two brothers, about how each of the prisoners, ma'am, had escaped with stretcher and everything, even though they were in chains, and how the guard, fully armed, had been forced to act in self-defense, and how the body, ma'am, had somehow managed to end up, hanging from a tree on the other side of the hill, ten kilometers from the hospital from which the escape attempt had been made; since his brothers were only two of the many who at nightfall found themselves arrested in one place and at dawn turned up dead someplace else, or who disappeared in front of their houses and later died on some deserted beach; since his captors intended to kill him anyway, Theo knew what he had to do; scarcely had they tied his body, already blue from the cold and the bruises, to the stretcher and left him alone with his burned skin and broken ribs, than he decided to escape from there that very night.

It would have been difficult to distinguish anything in that darkness, nor was the only eye he could open, swollen and red, any help at all, but he discovered that his hands could feel their way and reach down to the swinging ends of the chains and tie a knot in them, and that this allowed him to drag, pull, move the bed inch by inch, for in fact, just as the report on his brothers had said, the stretcher did have wheels.

He pushed aside the thought that tomorrow they would exhibit him to a flock of reporters as irrefutable proof that prisoners really did try to escape under the most perilous conditions. They were going to apply the Fugitive Prisoners Law to him anyway, in the back and with painfully believable bullets, no matter what he did. He couldn't go on waiting eternally for those authoritarian footsteps in the hallway, waiting to be carted off, bed and all, and his chest blown outward into a thousand pieces, without even a wall to stain, held up by the same rusty frame of the same stretcher where they had liquidated his brothers. He had waited enough— every day, in that cellar where they had him blindfolded, every day of what had seemed an endless century, for the arrival of someone with a vulture's breath and a vulture's claw and a vulture's eternal hunger, who would descend on his body as if he were already a corpse and the only thing left to the bird was to gnaw his liver and devour his lips and twist his bones, feeding on his screams, and tomorrow, the same thing again at the same time, and the next day, waiting, waiting. Inside, where that hunger could not reach, he kept telling himself that he had nothing to repent of, that he assumed full and sole responsibility for what he had accomplished with millions of others. And outside he could hear his mouth whispering that he admitted organizing the union, that he had helped to take over the factory because it belonged to those who worked it, that he had then used these hands, now shackled, to tear down the flyers announcing the curfew and that he had indeed then initiated a hunger strike because half the workers at the plant were being fired. And inside: I admit I'm a man and proud of it.

But that was all they got out of him—and not one name, not one address, not one other confession—and so, filled with his words that were of no use to them, the interrogators, still hungry for him, for the next prisoners, for the cell which must be emptied, had moved him to this hospital to finish him off.

In its official report the military said that his brothers, each on his own and a week apart, had managed to reach the hallway, that they had strangled the guard with their sheets, and then, with their cots chained to their backs, had crammed themselves into one of the unguarded elevators. It was all patently absurd—but who was going to investigate or point out the contradictions in that official version? According to the statement by the Army, and the sparse paragraphs in the newspaper, that's what his brothers had done and, then, quietly, lubricating the wheels of their beds with their own saliva so no one would hear them in the hospital's main corridor, they had knocked out two more guards and stolen their guns, forcing them to call an ambulance so that they might escape into the wilderness of the nearby city. It had unfortunately been necessary, the colonel was quoted as saying at the press briefing, to shoot them down to prevent them from continuing their terrorist rampage against the peace-loving citizens of this beloved land.

But standing before the coffin of each of the victims, Theo had told himself that it wasn't true, that his brothers had not even suspected the soldiers would take them to a hospital in order to execute them. And yet that is exactly what had happened: after shooting them in cold blood, they had invented the great escape story that his brothers, of course, were not in a position to deny. And Theo had sworn that when his turn came, soon enough because he was the oldest remaining son in the family and the obvious next name on the list, they weren't going to kill him for having waited, that he would in fact surprise them by acting out the ridiculous tale, step by step, just as the Colonel had recounted it.

That's why he was slithering out into the hallway now with his whole body cramped from the effort and—what do you know—the corporal was in fact sleeping peacefully, just as he had been supposedly when each of Theo's brothers had slipped out of their rooms, because the man could not imagine a prisoner trying to make such an inconceivable getaway. So it wasn't that hard to work the stretcher around ever so silently so that its head would be opposite the soldier who guarded the exit with his snores, and then to use those chained hands to extend the hospital sheet and suddenly, violently, pull it tight around the throat that was now struggling to breathe, as the eyes bulged and in terror recognized the prisoner through the haze of his lungs heaving for air, unable to convince himself that breathing could be so impossible when you're being strangled by an invalid tied to a stretcher and that the death that was happening to him was what the lying official versions were proclaiming had already happened to him several months ago, except that now he was really being killed, now his tongue was hanging from his mouth, something in his torso was desperate to break away from the murky water in which it was sinking, and he tried to play dead so that those mutilated arms would at least leave him alone, but they kept on squeezing his neck until he would never need to play anything anymore for any audience whatsoever.

Theo stared at the fallen corporal as though he couldn't believe that this was not a TV murder, a scene from a docudrama that somebody else was filming. But that first hurdle had been jumped. Now—on to the elevator.

Everything had already been written in the bureaucratic report they had given him and his mother. That was how Theo knew that the service elevator would be run by a corpulent sergeant whom he could not possibly surprise. It was, on the other hand, feasible to use the public elevator, although he could only get the stretcher in diagonally, as the Colonel had made clear to him when he expressed some doubt, using drawings and arrows, as if it had been a geometry lesson dealing with rectangles rather than with the simulated deaths of his brothers. His jailers, therefore, were orchestrating his escape; they were the ones who had unwittingly researched and explained the hospital schedule, the changes of guards, the dimensions of the elevators and the stretchers with the intention of making his brothers' false escapes fit into and conform to that real functioning structure. To make his way through this labyrinth he had only to follow those fraudulent instructions to the letter, let the military guide him to freedom.

And what if they caught him? What if the walls of that hospital were one big net of recording devices and magnetic eyes? What if all this was just a scheme to justify all past and future shootings, and he was playing into their hands? What if tomorrow they exhibited a film of his escape as proof that, like himself, the others had undertaken the impossible—and his final fate was to be used to silence those who refused to believe the official lies?

Theo's only response was to press the elevator button angrily. If a bullet rips through my flesh, I'll have made them waste one more bullet; we'll have made them run, sweat, fear, before we died, and I'll remain swimming in their pupils like a wild stallion that keeps on galloping in someone's memory years after its flanks have been ripped and torn to shreds. If they're watching me, if they're taking snapshots, if it's all a game, that's all right; because my brother or somebody's brother will come next, his sretcher and his chain and his firing squad awaiting him—but not these chains, not the ones I'm wearing, they'll have to replace these, I'm not going to give them back, we're going to steal all the stretchers in the world. When it's the next brother's turn, he'll just have to learn that the way out must be through the back staircase or jumping from a window and hanging from the tree limbs like an orangutan, but that there is an escape, somewhere there has to be an unguarded passage.

With their deaths, their real deaths and their reported deaths, Theo's brothers had tested the first fallible routes, revealing in a roundabout way the nets in which the military wanted to trap each member of the family, and Theo knew that he had to try, because if it wasn't his flight, it would be someone else's, if he didn't succeed today, then someone would find the way tomorrow, until finally one man would reach the outside world with the message that not only was it possible to escape but that millions of us will be doing it, melting the rifles in the hands of the executioners, hiding inside boxes of rotting garbage, disguised as doctors or as their patients, feigning death and finally not dying in the attempt.

He had to stand up in order to prepare his entry to the public elevator, sideways, the way he was trying it now, with his back bent like a farm laborer harvesting somebody else's wheat, a task for which his life's work had prepared him and now permitted him to survive in spite of the agony in his beaten shoulders. There he was, despite the chains, half-lifted, bent like some Indian ancestor carrying the conquistadors through Andean passes, like some broken ancestor dragging a colossal cannon across the deserts to serve in wars he did not understand, like some mining ancestor coughing his way along the tunnels in search of the coal that would provide the fuel to drive ships which he would never board, carrying his load, now with all the strength inherited from those two brothers who had not tried and been murdered anyway, from those great-grandfathers who had tried and died miserable deaths just the same. When the door slid open, he fell into the elevator as if the past were falling with him and holding him up at the same time, because the elevator wall took some of his burden and he knew that he would be able to rest against the chains and his drooping head was half an inch from the ground-floor button and his forehead pressed it, even though that meant the bleeding would start up again as the elevator door started to close and it was good not to see the corporal lying on his back at the end of the hall, looking at the sky as if he were praying. No, he could rest now, as the elevator descended, plan his next step, the nurse busy with her work so she would not interfere, the guards at the end of the lobby near the side door, their backs to the elevator, just as the Colonel had explained it to his mother and to him: of course, young man, they had their backs to the elevator, don't you see, their job is to watch the entrance, not to suppose that some scrawny prisoner has managed to get to the ground floor; that's why your first brother's plan and your second brother's plan were so diabolical, young man, because they caught the guards unprepared. But your sons, ma'am, were polished off anyway. Nobody gets away, however smart he thinks he is.

And, in effect, there they were, backs to him, at the end of the shining linoleum, beyond the sickly sweet and poisonous and slightly acid odor of anesthesia which always hung there, beyond the nurse who doesn't look up from her desk where she is filling out forms, exactly as the Colonel had described the scene, and it's incredibly easy to reach the two soldiers without making a sound, to cross the hall and get behind them and now, out of view of the nurse, just at they said his brothers had done, to take the sharp end of the chain—yes, young man, they were careful not to let it clink—and stick it into the backs of the soldiers as if that link of chain were the barrel of a revolver, the same chain that also bound his brothers—and finally to take the guards' weapons.

No, young man, they could not have unbound the chains. Those soldiers did not have the key—and to shoot the chains off would have alerted the whole building, so your brothers had an ambulance called.

This was the moment of truth, the critical point, the moment to abandon the written script, because to get into an ambulance was to be handed over to death. He now must find the way to escape not only from the hospital, but from the story of his brothers' deaths. So Theo orders them to call for the ambulance, blindfolds them, and when it arrives, orders them to climb into its pure white vaults, just as the Colonel had predicted—as if this were one of those World War II movies. But he does not climb in after them, as the movie would have him do. Grunting and cursing, he lifts another stretcher up into the ambulance, corners them with it, tells them in a hoarse voice to go north, in the direction of the gully on the far side of the city where his brothers had been found, and lets them know that it would be a pleasure to spatter the immaculate ambulance walls with their brains, if they have any—and watches with satisfaction as they howl off into the night, supposedly carrying him as they had supposedly carried his brothers.

And now he was finally riding inside words that had not been pronounced by that Colonel. If his two brothers had taken that ambulance, ma'am, each one at his own risk, if they had been unfortunate enough to be mowed down by machine-gun fire against the fence, Theo, on the other hand, was using the rifles like oars to row his boat, his sailing bicycle, toward the south, building up speed as if they were two magic crutches, two big brothers coming to the rescue in the best fairy tale tradition, and he were some giant eternally chained to a rock. But this wasn't that idiotic rock that had to be pushed infinitely up a hill only to roll down again and then pushed up once more; if it was a rock at all it was a rock made of man, his chains turned into arms, a rock that did not repeat the errors of the past, a rock that had stolen life's flames and dared to pass them on, that was not going to wait for some liberator's hands to come from far away to send it on its way, a rock that would be used to build something useful once it got to the top of the hill or the end of the grounds, where perhaps, after all—and Theo dismissed the thought for the last time—a legion of machine guns awaited him in order to take a final photograph.

They weren't waiting for him.

At that very moment he heard how machine guns riddled the ambulance far to his north, how they opened its doors and the empty stretcher fell out, hurling its fractured pieces of bedding at the feet of the soldiers as they approached, reloading their guns, and the Colonel was smiling, one more brother trapped, one more pig on his way to the market, while Theo's stretcher, the real one, with him aboard, made its way through the unguarded woods, his wheeled, almost winged, stretcher, his forearms scarred and proud, finally sure that the Colonel had not told the truth and would be realizing right now as he contemplated the absent body that he was going to have to call Mama and instead of smugly notifying her that her third son had been caught, like the other two deceased, trying to escape the hospital; instead of lamenting the fact that the forces of order had been left no other choice than to use their firearms; instead of inviting her to identify and weep over the lonely and naked remains in an unfurnished room—instead of this story the Colonel would take a deep breath and would stare at Mama, while Theo escaped into the darkness like a wondrous animal endowed with more arms and legs than he knew what to do with, flowing in the river of himself and the stretcher, fleeing beneath the blue stars far from the barking dogs and the faraway fury of the inquisitors, fleeing impossibly, impossibly driven by the words with which the Colonel would have to inform Mama, the words that he would have to extract from himself, tooth by tooth, words that had never been planned, that were not in the basement of any report, not in any manual his advisers had loaned him to perfect his studies, those words that only I had anticipated like a bonfire brought to the rest of the world to teach it not to be afraid of the dark; and I listen to those cutting, definitive, glorious words that the Colonel spits at Mama, trying to bite them before they are born into the universe, proving that nobody is dreaming me, that nobody has the right to tell my story but me, the words the Colonel did not release to the press, those words that I am forcing him to state, as if I were kicking them out of his mouth, those words which to Mama will mean that I may be wounded, but that I am whole, and that someday we have a chance of winning, we have a chance of telling this story our way, those words that are, after all, so simple:

"All right, ma'am, tell us once and for all, where's your son Theo hiding? He just gave us the slip."

BACKLANDS

for
José
Zalaquett

And yet here I am, still defending the castle.

They have told me that of the city nothing is left. I haven't had the stomach to turn around and look. But it cannot be that all was destroyed: in the breeze that hits my back, there is a hint of green, the hope of something fresh. Listen carefully. That rustling of tiny shrunken creatures drinking, almost melted by the heat, but drinking from what must be hidden wells. And other sounds: someone making a pathway, the way a bell calls a bell even though both are crushed into the mud. Let others suggest those shadows beyond the flames are the wind stirring dead ashes. I know that they are hands and I know that they gather wood. Soon I will hear the first shelters being rebuilt secretly, secretly. That is why I have not left these ramparts which are now our only home. I roam them endlessly with my face turned toward the hills where the enemy's artillery continues to blast what remains of the city behind me and makes it tremble. I will not watch what is being done. As long as I cannot avoid what is being done, I will not watch it.

They say my brother left. Others have sworn he is dead. I cannot be sure who is right. I have no time for the pain of his absence. Only time for my eyes to endlessly scan the dirty forests where the enemy watches and tries to discover, with compasses, with calculations, the location of these castle walls.

Were the enemy to find me, there would be no one left to remember the old elm tree under which I first saw the stars, gave them names. And if the tree has fallen before the axe, if the house where I was born is now rusting, sinking into a swamp, I would rather not know it. There are some that ask me to turn around, to accept once and for all the magnitude of what has befallen us. Nothing is left, they tell me. So we should take our families or what's left of them and leave this valley. They ask me to accept the fact that this city will be nothing more than a pleasant memory that will well up when the wine is too warm in our throats and we start to sing the old hymns that our grandchildren may identify and repeat but will not understand. They say that now we have to let this city occupy its only possible dimension, in still lifes from another time, sold outside second-rate inns, or in maps designating streets that were bombed and that—now passed into oblivion— perhaps never existed. That's what they say.

I'm not denying our losses. The gardens are filled with garbage, the air is rotting, even the trees smell like some sort of dark sperm stuck to the earth. Why should I deceive myself, like others: when an orange has been defiled, when a book is burned, the light will never whiten again in exactly the same way. But something can be done. When the mist descends and shrouds me, I can hurl my voice at them, so the enemy will at least be afraid, will wonder if we are coming back some day, if we will start to pick up, as I do, the scent of a jacaranda blossom still there, still somewhere. To block forever that trace of a fragrance wafting toward them, they will flood the city, they will try to drown my memories. But I will not watch the water. The sight of it could convince me that the scent of flowers I pick up, weak, so far away, is false. If I accepted the existence of that water, if I looked into its depths, I'd have to gather my belongings and leave. I'd have no choice but to leave, I tell you. So do not ask me to turn around. For me that hour has not come— and maybe never will.

"Stubborn man," she dares to say. "This is the last castle left and you're the last defender. The others have gone. And your brother has forgotten you."

A time will come for that, too. A time when I can tell myself, or hear someone else tell me, that perhaps the city was never as luxuriant as I remember it. Yes, that even back then, in that jubilant time before the enemy came, the sun was relentless and harsh in certain neighborhoods where not a park had been opened, not a tree was given the chance to grow.

"The only place the city exists is in your head," she tells me.

She says that, yes, but she stays here at my side. Chewing on roots, sipping filthy rainwater, mending old and wrinkled curtains so we can cover ourselves, she will stay here beside me, a second wall in the defense.

"Not just my head," I correct her. "Not just mine."

Beyond the ruined drawbridge and the road that leads to our dwelling, birds die in mid-flight, vainly searching for their wings in some moment of the air, and they hang on to the illusion, as they drop violently to the earth, that the shadow they are meeting is their own companion, another bird come to protect them. So I say nothing. My only answer, when it is not dangerous, is to make a torch flicker and burn—the way people used to in normal times so ships wouldn't run aground on the reefs, so pilgrims could find us and share some bread at our table. This is all that she has left, my way of lighting the night so a messenger can come, the way in which my shoulders refuse to accept the declining light, the way in which I have not allowed the horizon to disappear. And as long as I don't move from this place, she will be here, she will defend the castle by my side.

Every night, before making my rounds, I visit her. I lead myself gropingly to the tower where she rests, and there she receives me. Ravaged as she was the day I found her, as eroded as the house where she had taken refuge. She is, she told me—or perhaps it was somebody else—she is my brother's wife. I cannot be sure, because not even that first time did I want to run my fingers over her face. She, or somebody else, told me her face is empty and barren.

"They burned it on purpose, bit by bit, so nobody would recognize me."

She asked me to look at it; she stepped out of the shadows of the doorway so I would have to look at her face. I shut my eyes tightly and I placed both hands on the place where her cheeks should have been, where her forehead, her eyebrows, her lips should have been. I felt the face below me as if it were an island of ice floating on a wasted area.

"Look at my face," she said.

My hands moved lower, to her neck. I dared imagine it white in the intense darkness. I concentrated on filling my mouth with the memory of a ripe apple. I would undress her the way a farmer harvests wheat under a storm, with absolute faith that one seed will be saved, even though he knows the crop will be ruined.

"No," she said. "No, not that way."

How could I explain that I couldn't make love to her, that I didn't want to, that it was impossible. Yet my hands, as if of their own accord, descended to her belly. They needed to go on touching her that way, from a distance, without the rest of my body interfering. It was necessary to explore, however remotely, the cleft of her sex, what had once been the music of her thighs, almost as if I were somebody else. Somewhere my hands would discover the child in us that softens and flows, that hidden place we might still become.

"It's not good like that; it you don't look at my face, it's no good."

She takes one of my hands and guides it toward her head once more. Here and there her hair has started to grow in again. Soon she'll have enough to stream in the wind—and then the invaders will come again and, if they find her, this time they will start at the roots, deep down into the scalp they will start, and who knows if it will grow once more, one more time.

"You're cheating," she told me. "Not like that."

I stayed there motionless, listening for a while to the rhythmic beating of her heart, thinking about the newness with which her lungs filled and emptied, the precise miracle of her muscles that went on obeying commands. What else was inside her, untouched, territorial, clean, that someone might explore someday?

All of a sudden, her tone changes. She asks about my brother. Just like that, with no warning. "They say they saw your brother among the ruins of the monastery. They say he was dragging himself along the walls. That's what they say."

They say many things about my brother.

When his eyes are here once more beside me, when I see him approach these walls I have defended, when we can show him the meadowlands born beneath the scorched alleys, when he sees the new city that the young began to build on the ruins of the old one, or next to the old one, between, beyond, inside, above, beneath, in the very spaces between desecrated tombs, while I remained stubbornly there on the walls, shielding from the enemy the sounds of seeds my brother once planted, that he once planted but will not see grow . . .

"And these children?" my brother will ask.

"They're yours, brother."

"And this way of gathering the grain? And the caution in your footsteps? Why so serene? Where did you learn to forgive but not to forget?"

"It's the way we are, brother. It's a gift to you."

"You've changed."

"Yes. There are some things we've learned in these years."

It's cold up here on the castle walls. I lie down beside her, braced against the stone. It's not bad living here, near a woman's warmth, untroubled by what I cannot watch. I open my eyes and, beyond the woman, I contemplate that gray zone out in the hills where the enemy sleeps but does not rest.

"Can you have children?" I ask her.

"Why don't you ask me if I want to have children?"

"Can you have them?"

"You sent messengers," she answers, and her hands engulf me like warm rags, trying to protect my back from the savage wind, from the sorrow that bites in the wind as if it came from the past. "You sent messengers and they got lost."

Once again my hands move fleetingly between her legs and climb to her breasts and, as usual, glide upward toward her face but then, avoiding it, descend once more.

"Your brother will pass us by," she tells me. "Like all the others, he'll think there's nobody here anymore. Even the enemy believe, they proclaim that the castle has been abandoned."

"The enemy know I'm here."

I stopped, anticipating a certain irony, a note of tender mocking: "Of course. You're here. You still defend the castle."

". . . and that others are doing what they can," I finished.

"Where are the men you sent away with messages?"

It's true. I sent men to let the outside world know I was here. To let them know that the city might be in ruins but that in the hidden nearby castle someone was still on the ramparts. Runners had come, bearing ill tidings: our last garrison has fallen, in every castle across our land the time of the knives has come, the time of the knife against the menace of a throat, the time of the boot searching out the exact spot in the backbone. The last emissaries to come through did not say a word. They merely took off their capes and left them, waving fruitlessly or perhaps heroically in the wind. It was the horizon which brought final confirmation. For days the mountains disappeared behind the smoke of shattered glass, a curtain of black ice which would not evaporate and would have disheartened the strongest of warriors.

I held out. Not because I was braver than the rest. Perhaps because I was luckier. But mainly because it was the only thing I could do. Later the time would come, and will come, to find out how many more, like myself, defended the lemons in the grove, how many of us are still holding out in this valley, unable to see each other from hill to hill, how many rebuilt ramparts will emerge when the fog clears. There must be somebody else—the sounds that reach me from afar can only be human. Their very cadence assures me there are survivors, underground armies gathering.

In my own city, they swore there was no one left, that night of the invasion, while the bridges crumbled and the ships sank. It was then that I decided not to leave.

I had already turned my back on the city.

"How many of us are left?"

"Nobody," was the answer. "Just one moon, scavenging and dying there in the ashes. Let us flee, Captain."

Just the moon? Just one moon, and ashes. Then where do these arrows I am shooting come from? Where did I get the clothes that cover me, barely, barely? Cloth was needed, and needle and thread, and a hand and an eye to sew—and this food, this softness of honey, this cracker—and this beginning of a roof, who is behind all this?

"It's not good like this. Not without looking at me. No."

The enemy cannot see those who nourish me, nor can I. If I turned around I would contemplate only a desolate, sick-faced steppe. But the others have done what they could, what they were told to do. If the invader comes, kneel beside the bard, near the bonfire, gather up all the sacred songs and sing them in a secret voice until they cannot be forgotten, bid the bard farewell with reverence because he will soon lie in a mass grave—and with your thousand oars try to reach a river where you can keep the melodies for a day when they can be heard by all. To others: tend to the wounded, save medicine that may be needed ten years hence. Still others were to take care of the children or save one hammer, just one hammer and perhaps some nails. I didn't get the worst job: think about those who must spy on the enemy, eat in his kitchen, kiss his women and smile at his jesters. Think about those who descended into the deepest pit of the most remote prison to witness what was being done, to tell with a clear voice what some hoarse crawling bird has gone through inside. To me they said: don't surrender this castle.

"Even if they destroy the city?"

"Don't surrender the castle."

I never received a counterorder.

"Captain, the city is burning."

For a single instant, I was tempted. How good it would be to lift anchor. We would make for other valleys, unmoored at last, evading the eye in the center of the enemy's spyglass. Behind us the invaders would arrive late, would look for the castle and see only our misty silhouettes, disappearing in the distance. Perhaps someday we would return, falling upon them like a plague of pirates.

"Let us flee, Captain."

To someone else they may have said: leave as soon as it starts, look for refuge, tell our friends what happened, send food, send gloves for the winter, return as soon as you can. Perhaps still others were afraid. As for me, they had told me not to move an inch.

The city's savage breath beats at my back, like an oven lit by a man gone insane. It was then I decided not to turn around. The fire would die out, finally there would be nothing left to burn. The flames would lap at my walls, like bound, like tamed ocean waves. Let the enemy squeeze the city till it was only a rind. Could not a new fruit be dreamed from the peelings? Some house would be left standing, a church, a stable or two, a carpenter's bench. How could there be no one left who would know how to teach the alphabet? Some paper on which to write?

It's time to make my rounds. I stand up. I attempt to cover her with what's left of my coat. I look toward the countryside, toward the sea and toward the snowcapped mountains. And what if my brother really doesn't come? What will happen then?

She isn't sleeping.

"Look at me. I want you to look at me once and for all." She stands up and blocks my view of the landscape with her face. I close my eyes. I have to close them. "I'm burned all over. Look at me, coward. I have no teeth. Look what they did to my breasts. Do you really think I can nurse a child? Do you really think there's any hope?"

I say yes, that in spite of everything, yes, I believe there is hope.

"When your brother comes by, he won't even recognize the walls. The garden we planted yesterday. The new wharf, for smuggling. The new names on the streets. He'll speak a different language."

What is she trying to tell me? It's not as if she wanted to leave. Why is she so insistent about my brother? Why does she ask about the messengers who don't return? Why does she pick up on everything that is twisted, mistaken and broken? Why are you so hard, my love?

"And if he were to pass by," she says, "and not see a thing?"

I search for an answer. I who defended the last source of water, who kept the enemy from uprooting the last fruit trees and tossing them into the flames, I who made love like a mollusk among the rocks and rains and with no pleasure, I who breathe our daily poison so there will be a sun next morning, so the sun won't forget to come up from behind the mountains each morning, so there will not be darkness forever, so that one day the pieces of this puzzle shredded by an insane mind will settle back into place, I who defended the castle, I search for an answer.

If he were to pass by and not see us? If he were to forget the road back? If he had formed another family across the sea?

I'll watch him pass by. From up here, I'll see his figure appear. My eyes are used to distinguishing even the slightest movement. I'll see him.

"But if he passes by," she insists, "and doesn't recognize me? If he says, 'And who's this woman? And this burned face, this faceless face?' If he says, 'She's ugly.' What if he doesn't recognize me, what then?"

Then the moment will have arrived. I'll call the child we have made. I'll call the nephew my brother didn't see born.

"Do you see that man? Do you see that man riding off on a horse?"

FOR THE BEST IN PAPERBACKS, LOOK FOR THE

In every corner of the world, on every subject under the sun, Penguin represents quality and variety—the very best in publishing today.

For complete information about books available from Penguin—including Pelicans, Puffins, Peregrines, and Penguin Classics—and how to order them, write to us at the appropriate address below. Please note that for copyright reasons the selection of books varies from country to country.

In the United Kingdom: For a complete list of books available from Penguin in the U.K., please write to *Dept E.P., Penguin Books Ltd, Harmondsworth, Middlesex, UB7 0DA.*

In the United States: For a complete list of books available from Penguin in the U.S., please write to *Dept BA, Penguin, Box 120, Bergenfield, New Jersey 07621-0120.*

In Canada: For a complete list of books available from Penguin in Canada, please write to *Penguin Books Ltd, 2801 John Street, Markham, Ontario L3R 1B4.*

In Australia: For a complete list of books available from Penguin in Australia, please write to the *Marketing Department, Penguin Books Ltd, P.O. Box 257, Ringwood, Victoria 3134.*

In New Zealand: For a complete list of books available from Penguin in New Zealand, please write to the *Marketing Department, Penguin Books (NZ) Ltd, Private Bag, Takapuna, Auckland 9.*

In India: For a complete list of books available from Penguin, please write to *Penguin Overseas Ltd, 706 Eros Apartments, 56 Nehru Place, New Delhi, 110019.*

In Holland: For a complete list of books available from Penguin in Holland, please write to *Penguin Books Nederland B.V., Postbus 195, NL-1380AD Weesp, Netherlands.*

In Germany: For a complete list of books available from Penguin, please write to *Penguin Books Ltd, Friedrichstrasse 10-12, D-6000 Frankfurt Main I, Federal Republic of Germany.*

In Spain: For a complete list of books available from Penguin in Spain, please write to *Longman, Penguin España, Calle San Nicolas 15, E-28013 Madrid, Spain.*

In Japan: For a complete list of books available from Penguin in Japan, please write to *Longman Penguin Japan Co Ltd, Yamaguchi Building, 2-12-9 Kanda Jimbocho, Chiyoda-Ku, Tokyo 101, Japan.*

"Yes, Papa."

"Do you see him clearly?"

"Yes, Papa."

"That man is your uncle."

"Yes, Papa."

"Someday he's going to come back this way and you're going to call him 'Uncle.' I may not be here . . . what will you call him?"

"I'll call him 'Uncle.' "

And then, taking my son by the hand, I will let my brother disappear into the distance. And then, yes, at that moment, I will turn around to look our city in the face.